dictionary of modern anguish

FICTIONS BY

R. M. BERRY

FC2

Normal/Tallahassee

Published by FC2 with support provided by Florida State University, the Unit for Contemporary Literature of the Department of English at Illinois State University, the Program for Writers of the Department of English at the University of Illinois at Chicago, and the Illinois Arts Council

Address all inquiries to:
Fiction Collective Two, Florida State University
c/o English Department, Tallahassee, FL 32306-1580

ISBN: Paper, 1-57366-085-X

Library of Congress Cataloging-in-Publication Data

Berry, R. M.
    Dictionary of modern anguish:fictions by / R. M. Berry.--1st ed.
        p. cm.
    ISBN 1-57366-086-8 -- ISBN 1-57366-085-X (pbk.)
    1. Experimental fiction, American. I. Title

PS3552.E748 D5 2000
813'.54--dc21

                                            00-025819

Cover Design: Polly Kanevsky
Book Design: Tara Reeser

Produced and printed in the United States of America
Printed on recycled paper with soy ink

Illinois ARTS Council
AN AGENCY OF THE STATE OF ILLINOIS

This program is partially sponsored by a grant from the Illinois Arts Council

dictionary of

modern

anguish

acknowledgments

THE AUTHOR WISHES TO THANK
THE EDITORS OF THE FOLLOWING
JOURNALS IN WHICH EARLIER
VERSIONS OF SEVERAL OF THESE
STORIES FIRST APPEARED.

NEW ORLEANS REVIEW
    ("SECOND STORY")
FIVE POINTS
    ("MIMESIS")
APALACHEE QUARTERLY
    ("TORTURE!")
FICTION INTERNATIONAL
    ("THE SENTENCE")
THE MASSACHUSETTS
REVIEW
    ("HISTORY")
    [REPRINTED IN
    A GOOD DEAL:
    SELECTED STO-
    RIES FROM *THE
    MASSACHUSETTS
    REVIEW*, ED. MARY
    HEATH AND FRED
    MILLER ROBINSON]
THE MINNESOTA REVIEW
    ("THE FUNCTION OF
    ART AT THE PRESENT
    TIME")

THE AUTHOR GRATEFULLY AC-
KNOWLEDGES THE ASSISTANCE OF
AN INDIVIDUAL ARTIST GRANT
FROM THE FLORIDA DIVISION
OF CULTURAL AFFAIRS IN
THE COMPLETION OF THIS WORK.

for

JERRY BRUNS

The problems arising through a misinterpretation of our forms of language have the character of *depth*. They are deep disquietudes; their roots are as deep in us as the forms of our language and their significance is as great as the importance of our language. —Let us ask ourselves: why do we feel a grammatical joke to be *deep*? (And that is what the depth of philosophy is.)

Wittgenstein
PI §111

contents

a theory of fiction

Living with a secret, you measure time differently. Solitude becomes a still point, worlds pass at the speed of light. Perhaps it's feeling so immaterial that makes me want to speak, now that whatever I say is futile. I don't know. But approaching the end, I keep insisting, I was *there*! Or simply, I, I, I! But these words don't express these words. I'm writing as badly as I know how. I'd implore you to doubt everything, but you already do, and it isn't enough.

It has been nearly half a century since I invited Schreiber to lecture on my campus. We'd known each other briefly at Minnesota, but since graduation, I'd followed— and been deeply impressed by—his early articles on *Gil Blas* and *Quixote*. Schreiber's account of the novel was, of course, anathema to mine, but I was astonished that such alien procedures could share common grounds. I suppose I made his publications my personal test. Anyway, I was teaching seminars in what we then called the novel's "social history" and had introduced my students to his work. I knew he'd be eager to come. We exchanged calls and letters; I agreed to play sponsor in the affair. More importantly, I offered him a place to stay in my home. I was living alone at the time, as I am now—my too brief but reasonably satisfying marriage having filled the intervening years—and I had a spare room for guests.

When Schreiber got off the plane, I was surprised by how unimpressive he looked. At Minnesota we'd been part of a group—mostly overdue doctoral candidates and the nervously untenured—that drank itself blind every Saturday night. I recalled him as an ordinary sort, clumsy, a little introverted, but with a cleverness that could surprise you. But seeing him clutch the rail of the exit ramp now, his head bobbing out from behind a woman's purse, I felt embarrassed. Some of this was undoubtedly his stature. During the intervening years, I'd come to think of Schreiber as the author of his writings, my adversary. I suppose I'd made him larger than life. But standing head to shoulder with ordinary mortals now, he seemed the picture of helplessness. His beard was ridiculously long. His trousers were miserably cut. Although my admiration for his genius has never wavered— I say this even now—his dismay at commonplace things was hard to accept. I recall in particular his bewilderment at the practice of checking luggage, some bitter remarks about his bag having been "confiscated" by the airline, and his subsequent amazement when I retrieved it from the baggage return. Perhaps I'm making too much of this. Anyway, Schreiber was only five feet tall.

I took him home, fed him, gave him a room. He put away his clothing, and then over brandy and a fire we settled down to discuss the subject we both loved—novels.

Schreiber's theory was as simple as it was audacious. He was convinced fiction didn't exist. The concept of fiction was created in the seventeenth century to distract us from our own absence. All stories—from the farthest-fetched to the most carefully documented—were actually confessions, and novelists were continually discovering this. Narrative genres could be differentiated by degrees of indirection, the modern novel being of all classes the most devious, but in Schreiber's view, nothing untrue had ever been told.

In my view, Schreiber's theory was reckless and naive, even socially irresponsible. Oh hell, I thought it was just crazy. Like virtually all of my contemporaries, I'd been impressed by the advance of science. Psychology, linguistics, historicism, were the vocabulary of intellectual seriousness. I suppose I had a vague notion of myself as a progressive. But Schreiber treated the material world as just another abstraction. I didn't want to challenge this view. I wanted to shake him back to his senses, jeer, C'mon, man! Not that I thought this would make any difference. Hadn't I read his essays? Couldn't I see how unbalanced he was? But that was just the problem! All I remember now is how little of what I said that night sounded like what I meant to say, as if my words were my words only as long as I didn't say them, or as if they were the words I wanted to say but never to *hear* myself say.

Anyway, I have little memory of our conversation. I think I chattered on about population shifts and the spread of commerce. Schreiber made some remarks about Locke but was plainly bored. Thank God for the brandy. However, I do remember one exchange. I don't know what had provoked me, but I'd started table-banging. I must've wanted Schreiber to admit that root canals in novels were preferable to root canals in dentists' chairs, or some such poppycock. Like I said, it wasn't me speaking. Finally I burst out with, "You aren't making me up, for Chrissakes! *This*"—and I struck myself on the chest—"*this* isn't fiction!"

Schreiber's face took on the queerest expression. His eyebrows dipped. His forehead wrinkled. He leaned forward and patted me on the arm. "You know," he said, "it's nothing to be ashamed of."

Eventually we gave up and went to our rooms. I fell immediately asleep. Several hours must've passed—I never checked the time—but I remember waking to the consciousness of someone very nearby. Suddenly, I heard my name called. Turning on the lamp, I saw Schreiber standing beside my bed, but with his features so exaggerated in theatrical horror that I almost guffawed.

"Catastrophe!" he blurted, and started jabbing his finger toward the guest room.

I must acknowledge a weakness. I am temperamentally averse to melodrama and, when confronted with histrionics, find myself inclined to sarcasm. Seeing the diminutive Schreiber in his nightshirt, his hair mussed, beard askew, eyes dilated, lips blathering, well, it was all I could do not to make a joke. "Bad dream?" I asked.

Schreiber merely grabbed my arm, said, "You must come…. Here, here!"

I allowed him to drag me to the guest room, where he halted in the doorway and gesticulated at the bed. I regarded his wadded up bedclothes with incomprehension. Schreiber offered no explanation. He merely stood there pointing at the sheets in a kind of magisterial rigidity, as if expecting me to understand. It was ludicrous! I was on the verge of losing all patience, and of telling him so, when I noticed something peculiar about his bottom sheet. I leaned forward, observing a slight transparency, flatness. I reached over, touched the place with my finger, sniffed. Then I knew. Schreiber had wet his bed.

Or rather, *my* bed. Well, it was a case, as Henry James would have said. I couldn't imagine how to react and would certainly have reacted badly had Schreiber not been there to show just how unpleasant a bad reaction in these circumstances could be. He was hopping from one foot to the other, wringing his hands, panting, making little snuffling noises, and generally looking like a candidate for euthanasia. A glance in his direction and I knew what I must do.

I swept up the bedclothes in my arms, admitting no flinch of repugnance, and instructed Schreiber to get rags and a sponge from the kitchen. I then stuck the sheets into the tub, turned on the water, wrung out the urine, soaped the affected areas, and tossed everything into the drier with the rest of the day's undried wash. I next set to exuberantly soaking and stanching the mattress, using the sponge and absorbent rags, and finally mixed a teaspoon of vinegar in a bowl of water for the coup de grace. I even sprinkled on a little baking soda, sweeping up the mess with a whisk broom, and finally covered over the dampness with a plastic bag. All this while I kept barking instructions to Schreiber. Fresh sheets in the hall closet! Deodorizer under the sink! Spot remover in the pantry! Of course, these activities were just diversions. I knew nothing of domestic chemistry and couldn't have said what, if anything, my measures were to accomplish. But so much bustle had the desired effect. Our attention remained fixed on the goal of reparation. Neither of us had to look the other in the face, neither had to admit that Professor Schreiber had just transgressed the most infantile of prohibitions.

By the time we stopped, everything was back to normal. To avoid awkwardness, I kept our parting crisp, mentioned the upcoming lecture, need for rest, etc. Since the business was so mundane, it could be treated as ordinary. We each returned to our room, and I tried to return to sleep, but my mind was now racing. I kept wondering whether this accident was habitual, whether Schreiber possessed some physical or psychic disability, like palsy or stammering, and if so, why he hadn't taken precautions. Why, knowing the possibility of such an embarrassment, would he agree to stay in my home? Why not safeguard himself with a hotel room? And if his failing were not habitual, how bizarre that it had occurred just now, while away from the bed in which he passed virtually every other night. Eventually I did get to sleep, but my rest was disturbed by a dream. In the dream I was seated at a game board in a huge auditorium playing a game no one had invented. My opponent countered my moves like an experienced player, and none of his moves seemed to perplex or startle me. However, whenever I studied the board, I saw only randomness and confusion. All at once I heard a loud voice: This day your shoes will be required of thee! I looked down at my feet and discovered I wasn't touching the ground. What has happened to Mother? I cried out. But the only reply was a thunderous laughter resounding in every direction. Then I realized: *this* too was part of the game! I turned back to the board, but my opponent was already completing his final move. You have lost, he announced. With a pang in my heart, I looked up to see who had defeated me. But I was alone.

I didn't decide, or not in the way one imagines making a decision—waffling, weighing alternatives, plopping down for this instead of that—I didn't decide how I should behave with Schreiber the next morning. It seemed a foregone conclusion that neither of us would bring up the previous night, a grotesque breach of decorum even to allude to it. But I suppose I expected some acknowledgment: a look, a pause before not saying what went without saying, or a vague remark that might be taken two ways. But no, there was nothing. We had the same breakfast, the same conversations, the same practical discussions—when to be where and could Schreiber use my carrel and would there be a chalkboard at the lecture—that we would have had in any case. I introduced my distinguished friend to colleagues and students, just as planned, and Schreiber displayed no unexpected reticence, none of the sinking equanimity that, really, you might have expected him to display. If anything, he seemed more self-possessed, less befuddled than the day before. Queerest of all, he seemed at ease with me. He was the center of attention, of course, while I was now in the supporting role. But for the first time I noticed the slightest tone of condescension in a few of his remarks—especially when senior colleagues were present—and at moments my invisibility felt strange.

Not that patronizing was unfamiliar to me. My friend's achievements were more impressive than mine, and gradations of scholarly respect were as much a fact of my life as differences in human height and longevity. It was just that towering a full foot above this person who, for all his deftness and precocity and gifts and verve, would never again be for me anyone who *wasn't* a bed-wetter...well, I suppose I found his insouciance to be fantastic. I felt an impulse to burst out laughing. Sitting beside him at the podium, it was all I could do not to nudge him in the ribs. I seemed hyperconscious that, at any moment, I could say, You'll never guess what happened to Professor Schreiber last night! I imagined the color draining from his face, his blathering lips, animal grunts, trembling hands. It was as though his dignity now appeared fraudulent, as if the previous night had revealed the truth, had stripped this impostor naked. The whim was crazy, but I had a powerful feeling that to be brought down was what he deserved.

Nothing else happened during Schreiber's visit. The lecture went off as planned, although I was personally disappointed. Schreiber's text was *Moll Flanders*, but his only contention seemed to be that Defoe's preface could be taken literally, that the novel was a pseudonymous autobiography just as its "editor" claimed. He made some extravagant remarks about Descartes, about discovering that one's own body could prove dubious, but his conclusions weren't surprising, and nobody appeared enthusiastic. Of course, my colleagues were polite. From the applause you might have thought Schreiber had been a hit, but watching my peers watching my friend, I wondered for the first time if I'd been taken in. My schoolmate was a witty and skilled raconteur, had a flair for sophistry, and possessed impressive learning, but his theory now struck me as shallow. I felt embarrassed for us both. Afterwards, we dined with a few faculty members at a local restaurant. Points from the talk were mentioned, but discussion never became vigorous. When I returned Schreiber to the airport, we spoke exactly as we would have spoken had his visit been a triumph. We parted vowing to stay in touch. I recall an unfamiliar feeling of lightness as I drove home. During a stretch of deserted highway, I rolled down my window and sang.

I never saw Schreiber again. Although we continued for several years to be members of the same organizations and to subscribe to the same journals and even to attend some of the same conferences, ours remained a phantom relation. I never ceased to be aware of him for a moment, and I have strong evidence that for many years, perhaps even until the end of his life, Schreiber thought about me viciously and often, but the climax of my tale has already passed. Throughout the prolonged denouement, my protagonist is absent, and this gives the plot a frustrated, intangible quality. By classical theories, it's broken-backed. If I'd been free to write as I pleased, of course, I wouldn't have plotted so ineptly. But whatever the case, the unraveling of my yarn got under way as soon as I returned from the airport and began to strip Schreiber's mattress.

He'd left no trace. Not that this seemed extraordinary in itself. I knew that, having been diluted, Schreiber's stain would be very slight—perhaps only a little urine actually passed through the sheet—but I did expect something: a slight discoloration, some dampness or watermark. I don't know. But the mattress was unblemished. Even the odor was indiscernible. I pressed down on the foam, cupped my hands about my nose, tried each nostril separately, finally pressed my cheek against the spot—or the *supposed* spot; exactly where, after all, was it located?—tried everything short of licking it, and still, no scent, no sign, nothing. Then it struck me. Schreiber had turned the mattress over! I flipped it, only to realize my explanation was impossible: the underside was ripped. I had purchased the mattress as a first year assistant and had taken advantage of a damaged merchandise sale. Had the mattress been turned over I would have seen, either last night or tonight, the duct tape I had used to contain the tiny crumbs of deteriorating foam. I dropped it back on the springs, but with a new misgiving. Why all this concern with details? It wasn't as if anyone were going to contest what I knew, or would even suspect it. I was behaving as if I were gathering evidence, trying to prove a point. I reminded myself that I could despise whomever I wished, was free to scorn Schreiber or Albert Schweitzer or the Buddha himself, if it struck my fancy. No justification would be required.

I went to bed, slept soundly, and thought no more about Schreiber or his preposterous accident for twenty-two hours—that is, until the very next evening while scanning an exhaustively researched and perfectly unreadable paper on *Hamlet* and the Irish wars, when I remembered: the sheets! I rushed down to the dryer, flung open the door—there was a ping of metal that later turned out to be the hinge snapping—and hauled out the linen. This time I had no difficulty locating a large stain, not clearly outlined but definitely yellowish, and of a plausible size, right in the middle of an otherwise unmarked top sheet. I will not describe how good this discovery made me feel, or how strange I felt to feel so. Even while undergoing my elation, still standing there before the machine with the sheet in my fist and the stain held triumphantly to my eyes, even as I all but skipped around the cellar with satisfaction, even as I now fear I actually did skip—even at that moment, I already heard the stranger who'd taken up residence in my consciousness hectoring me with questions about why, for Chrissakes, I was so worked up over a *stain*. I confess that I descended to the base ploy of arguing with him. I said that human curiosity was perfectly normal and that every natural phenomenon demanded an explanation. I also noted that, as a homeowner, I was responsible for all household damages and needed to replace any less than *comme il faut* appurtenances with new. Finally, I observed that anthropologists considered the ancient concern with cleanliness to be a ritualized behavior unrelated to modern theories of disease and that the human heart had reasons reason didn't know. I then told the stranger to shut up and leave me the fuck alone. I yanked the rest of the linens out of the dryer and began folding. I was ready to put Schreiber behind me.

It was then that I saw the second stain. Not on the fitted bottom sheet that made a pair with the first one, but on a second top sheet. Slightly more mustard-toned and faintly brown at the edges, it nevertheless looked interchangeable with the first stain, and seemed to be positioned in virtually the same place. The disturbance that came over me then is difficult to convey. I thought I would rip the fabric to bits. I feared I would do violence to myself. I longed for the sound of shattering glass, heard my teeth grind. I offer no explanations, but I know I experienced the kind of paroxysm that can be fatal to future repose. It was a crux. I felt frightened. I carried all the sheets from the dryer—two bottoms, three tops—into my living room and spread them out on the carpet. I had to move some furniture and place one corner over the threshold of the kitchen, but I finally managed to arrange the five side by side so that I could examine the data. I brought in the drafting lamp from my desk, turned on all the overheads.

The inspection required the larger portion of the night. No need to go into details. But my conclusion was that there were two stains, not entirely identical, but neither clearly announcing itself as urine instead of something else—coffee? dye? blood? jism? (I apologize for such frank excursions into the grossly physical, but reliable knowledge often demands nothing less.) Anyway, there were obvious differences but no difference that made the identity of either stain obvious. Both could be recent or old, both could be from food or excrement, both could be Schreiber's or mine or another's. The bed on which Schreiber slept had a top sheet and a fitted bottom one—I recalled this with clarity, or believed at the time that I recalled it with clarity, or believe now that I believed at the time that I recalled it with clarity—and so, had there been two stains, one should have been on a top sheet, the other on a fitted. This meant that either of the two stains before me could have been from Schreiber's mishap, consequently either could have been from an unrelated mishap, so that both could be cited in support of my case, so that neither could be cited in support of my case. At any given moment I might be staring at Schreiber's stain or at another stain whose origin was unknown. Moreover, inasmuch as neither bottom sheet—I am absolutely certain there was a fitted bottom sheet!—neither bottom sheet showed any stain at all, there was no sure evidence that Schreiber's urine *had left a stain*! It was quite possible that both stains were old, were mine, were peanut butter. In short, I knew nothing.

I got up from the floor and walked into the kitchen. It was five a.m. I cannot accurately convey my mood, but I recall feeling the proximity of a threat in its least mistakable form. I had to make a choice. There seemed to be an absolute but reasonless demand for action. My future hung in the balance. I gathered up all five sheets, loaded them into the trunk of my car, carried them to a supermarket three blocks away, and carefully stuffed them into a trash bin. I then returned home without resolving to act any differently, without reflecting on my intentions at all, but merely confirmed in a pattern of life from which the acknowledgment of Schreiber would be missing.

Two years passed during which I can say with frankness that I was at peace. Schreiber's visit was no more than a fact and so, like all facts, could be ignored. My life duplicated the life I would have lived if Schreiber had never entered my door. I continued revising my dissertation, a materialist poetics of eighteenth century genres (Defoe was my specialty), and published three chapters of it. In a single year I married my late wife, Dora, completed my manuscript, and received enthusiastic support for promotion and tenure. As long as the past could be restricted to my private knowledge of it, it differed in only trivial ways from a hallucination. Or as Schreiber would say, it passed for bad fiction. For it seems the real contribution of Schreiber's theory to draw attention to a familiar but unappreciated fact: that the best examples of fiction are inept ones. The classic novels, our paradigms, invariably confound and deepen our concept, often depriving us of recourse to it altogether. As a result, Schreiber maintained, we're continually falling back on pedestrian fabrications to reassure us that we're more palpable than a book. In my own case, I had transformed Schreiber's visit into a third-rate short story and so deprived it of any power to undo me. The only alteration in my otherwise unaltered existence was that I no longer read my adversary's writings. I couldn't have said why—that way madness beckoned. I merely accepted that my former friend's works were now among the plenitude I passed over.

If it wasn't the following year, then it was soon afterwards, that my fortunes took the downward plunge from which they've never recovered. Perhaps that way of introducing my denouement seems melodramatic. Of course, only my words can overcome the distrust my words arouse. If I forge on, it isn't blindly. I recognize the potential for self-defeat. I ask merely to be granted my self-awareness, my dignity. But then, why should you grant me anything?

Shortly after submitting my manuscript to a respected scholarly press, I received two enthusiastic, albeit not uncritical, reviews by senior scholars whose work I admired. Although revisions were requested, I sensed that a contract was in the offing and had begun a rewrite, when to my surprise a third set of criticisms appeared. As is customary, the author remained anonymous, but I was supplied with a copy of his remarks. Reading them made me dizzy. It wasn't any facts he (I always knew my adversary was male)...it wasn't my facts he disputed, or even my conclusions. His criticisms were fantastically trivial, a matter of mere diction, and at the same time so basic that I couldn't begin to accommodate them. He said I wasn't writing English. My "knowledge," he insisted, wasn't knowledge; when I spoke of "experience," I didn't mean experience; "material" in my text was immaterial; none of my references to "romance" or "idealism" referred to anything; I didn't know how the word "novel" was used, etc. It was as though nothing I wrote were anything I wrote, as though my text were a phantom of itself, unsentenced, or its own retraction.

I was outraged. This wasn't criticism! I insisted. It was annihilation! And my editors at the press were sympathetic. They encouraged me to submit a detailed and carefully reasoned refutation of the third reader, to urge the editorial board on defensible grounds to set his comments aside. I have difficulty explaining why I never did this. Perhaps it was my impatience at such distractions—I was deeply immersed in my rewrite—or perhaps I'd lost faith in the whole process, felt the press's respect for such a fool was damning. In retrospect, I suppose I should've followed the editors' advice, but I can recall how at the time such sensible suggestions only perfected my despair. For I didn't want to "refute" my third reader. I wanted him manacled. My overwhelming impulse was to wink at my scholarly peers, turn my finger in little circles beside my temple, join with them in an uproarious belly-laugh at this madman's expense. But "refute" him? Either it was just obvious that by "fiction" I meant fiction, not something else, or if it weren't obvious, then what could I say?

And so began the spiral of self-doubt that has kept me in revision for nearly fifty years. I submitted my manuscript to three more presses, each time receiving one or more favorable readings before my tormentor—I never doubted he was always the same—reappeared to silence me. It was, of course, Schreiber. Or if not Schreiber per se, then it was Schreiber in effect, virtually Schreiber. For even though the author's name was stricken from each review, even though my old schoolmate may not have been in the most doggedly literal sense "there," still my undoing could've been the work of no other. I often felt anger, even betrayal, but my feelings would never translate into an energetic defense. My experience never altered. After the rage subsided, after the confusion, well.... Schreiber's criticisms were ludicrous, mad, blind, wild, childish, inane, but what sense could there be in saying they were "wrong"?

I sound more bitter than I intend. In the end, the failure of my life's work wasn't Schreiber's fault. Contrary to what some claim, scholarship is no death struggle. In it there can be winners on many sides, and losses are rarely final. Although the confession causes me pain, I know that, had I persisted, had I risen to my tormentor's challenge, I might have emerged victorious in my own way. What defeated me wasn't Schreiber's theory. It was nothing. But that, I suppose, was Schreiber's theory.

For I simply couldn't believe the man's audacity: to challenge the one before whom his shame had been revealed! How was I to accommodate such brazenness, especially from someone so easily dismayed, someone as insubstantial as Schreiber? And then I began to be gnawed by what seemed obvious, that Schreiber really was *small*, smaller than I had ever dreamed, a desiccated little homunculus whose negligibility might prove infinite, in whose miniscule form the absence of vitality had produced longings so gnarled and inverse, so infantile, so loathsome.... The truth of it took my breath away: Schreiber had ruined me because I knew he was a bed-wetter! It was astonishing. And then the depth fully opened, the pit of my undoing. For I could see that to meet Schreiber's challenge I would have to preserve what would never bear repeating, to cherish my soiled sheets, dwell on the crudest, least significant corporeal remains— exactly as my madness had urged me to do years ago in the silence of my kitchen. I knew I wouldn't do it, that I would die with Schreiber's secret untold, that if I must choose between the facts and what mattered, I would always choose the other. And so I have protected Schreiber with my life.

And it is for this reason that, although Schreiber has died and my own public achievements ceased decades ago, I have been careful in telling my story to conceal Schreiber's true name. My last hope that someone somewhere will accord my misery the respect it craves, the respect that revealing it would have made impossible, is that I've given no one the power to injure my adversary with anything I've said. This has been proof of my faith. And it is for the same reason that I have carefully suppressed my own name in this account, so that no one could retrace through the neglected shelves of a forgotten library the sequence of events and identities I've been forced to relate. And I've even gone so far as to change the substance of our disagreements and the fields of inquiry in which we struggled, so that no one coming behind me might claim, oh, but he was only trying to win his grudge fight at the last, trying to blacken the name of his conqueror, smear the better reasoning when it could no longer respond. In reality, my enemy was six feet tall. And last, it has been in order to avoid the whole humiliating business of denial and deceit that I've disguised this true account of my suffering as the clumsiest of fictions.

second story

"Second Story" could have been an excellent novel. Its plot, or what remains of one, contains all the elements of which classic novels are made: a colorful locale, conflict among blood-kin, a background of immediate social and political interest. But the story we have is not that one.

A young man, I—, inherits his father's business, a small produce store. His sister, U—, is ignored in the will. Both siblings are living abroad at the time, and each reacts to the legacy with profound but mixed emotions. The sister despises her father (there are hints of sexual abuse) and hoped never to see him again. But being disinherited infuriates her. It replicates the injury done her as a child and revives the memories she crossed the ocean to escape. She undergoes a psychotic episode and ends up in a hospital in Scotland.

The son is living in Paris, pursuing his dream of becoming a writer, and failing utterly. He also hates his father. His reasons are unclear, but they may involve the father's abuse of his sister, for whom I— too harbors forbidden desires. However, I—'s anger is directed, not so much at his father as at his father's business. Or more specifically, at the apartment above it. It was in this flat, overlooking the street, that he and his sister were raised (the mother's absence is never explained). I— has a recurrent nightmare of being imprisoned there.

The inheritance takes on the character of fate for both siblings. I— is penniless and not especially strong. When the word of his inheritance reaches him, he is living on the charity of friends. It's wearing out. He badly needs a means of support, one that will allow him to practice his art, and he hasn't the faintest notion how to secure it. He obsesses about his father's legacy, feels himself being drawn back to America, rails at his weakness, et cetera.

This predicament is skillfully contrived, and for the first fifty pages or so, that is, until I—'s narration takes over, "Second Story" verges on being a captivating read. However, no sooner does I—'s writing become the novel's focus than its plot slows to, if not a halt, then a grind.

Part of the problem is that I— is afflicted with a debilitating self-consciousness of no obvious origin. He doesn't want what he wants, can't let himself do what he tries to do, questions everything. Once installed in his father's home, I— passes his days selling peaches and kumquats. He doesn't mind his father's business, even takes an interest in the daily accounts, but gradually he succumbs to repetition. He finds himself reliving old rivalries, waking to the sting of forgotten slights. One afternoon while washing rutabagas, he blurts out a schoolyard epithet. Later, counting change, he bursts into childish tears. He's able to compose himself only while sitting at his computer. Either he has been notified of his sister's breakdown or he has somehow fantasized it, but gradually he begins to narrate her ordeal from his vantage six thousand miles away.

U— passes her days in a tiny room with a window too high to see out. She experiences rages that exhaust her, prolonged episodes of sobbing and nightmares. Despite I—'s absence from these scenes, he describes her traumas with impressive vividness. U—'s symptoms are dramatized, and her interior monologue is convincing. There is a moving scene of masturbation.

In itself, the technique of substituting an imaginary account for a recollected one is neither confusing nor especially new and, if skillfully handled, can provide an effective variation in mood and tone. We willingly suspend our disbelief in I—'s point of view and allow ourselves to forget that, of course, he can't really imagine his sister's suffering. But unfortunately I— can't forget this. After describing U—'s memory of their father's voice, I— ruins his powerful effect by remarking, "Or this is how I picture U—." He continues narrating but now intersperses his story with expressions such as, "I seem to see her gazing up," or, "In my dreams he stifles her cries," or at his most ludicrous, "Is this the monstrous shape my hallucinations must all assume?"

Although irritating, these intrusions gradually become less noticeable, and for a time the narrative of U—'s recovery proceeds. In U—'s nightmare her father is perpetually inside of her. No matter how hard she struggles, she can never get free. U—'s doctor is a zombie, but a psychiatric resident comes alive to her plight. He explains to U— that she's creating her nightmares herself, that her father is powerless without her permission, that U— holds the key to her own jail. For some reason, this casts U— into the deepest gloom imaginable. She stops eating. Her eyes become expressionless. She spends whole days staring at a wall. Her breakthrough finally comes when one night she recognizes the violator of her dreams as the young psychiatrist. (This mistake is never explained.) She immediately begins to plot her escape from the hospital, feigning openness and recovered candor, and counting on the psychiatrist's sexual repression to make her scheme work. Despite I—'s tiresome asides, U—'s subterfuge makes for an exciting episode.

But the novel that "Second Story" might have been gets no further. One night while seated before his computer imagining U—'s torment, I— undergoes paralysis: "My fingers stopped," he recounts. "I stared into nothing. There across the waters I saw her raise her eyes, saw my hallucination looking back, saw U— seeing *this*." And we never find out how U— escapes the hospital. Instead we are treated to a two-page orgy of authorial self-loathing. ("How transparent I've become! All my designs, every pretense. Abasing U— just to exalt myself!") When next we hear of the sister, she's back in America.

At this point the novel starts to disintegrate. The narration fragments. The plot becomes contradictory. Increasingly, "Second Story" resembles a jumble of parts without plan or direction. Among the parts are: 1) I—'s unfinished narrative of U—, in multiple versions, with notes for a revision; 2) a self-serving autobiography about I—'s life as his father's heir (if there's any story in "Second Story," the autobiography concludes it); 3) seven journal entries, presumably written at a later time, disparaging both the narrative and the autobiography; 4) various documents about "Second Story" itself: a form rejection from an obscure press, an insipid jacket blurb, an anonymous reader's report (unfinished), and a review to which the author has attached his reply.

Needless to say, the reader finds this abandonment of artistic responsibilities infuriating. Presumably, the book's deterioration is meant to reflect the brother's worsening psychological state, but the more involved we become in the sufferings of U—, the more I— seems a distraction.

U— returns home and takes up residence on the street beside her father's, now her brother's, store. She shrieks at pedestrians, sleeps on the sidewalk, defecates in an adjacent alley. To all appearances she has become a lunatic. I—, meanwhile, is making a shambles of the business. Customers are leaving, creditors are phoning, everywhere there's the smell of rotten fruit. Then, seated at his computer one night, I— hears singing. At first he thinks he's a child again, then he decides he's asleep. Finally he goes to the window where he sees his sister's nude body swaying under a street lamp. The imagery turns evocative. He describes her "undulating trajectories, the fuchsia haze of darkness over my brain." He narrates his gradual loss of self-control, "as consciousness shattered on the cusp of her pain." He continues: "I saw the silver spike of moonlight, my sister's bare shoulders, her Gorgon's hair." He rushes downstairs. U— turns. Under a street lamp, brother and sister embrace.

Who knows what happens next? In the shortest of the ensuing fragments, U— and I— become lovers. They move back into their old room, where I— spends his days writing, while U— minds the store. At night they rejoin for exuberant fornication, made still more piquant by the taint of ancient taboo. I— (who in this fragment is narrating) says their union realizes his heart's deepest desire.

But gradually a feeling of uncanniness overtakes him, as if everything has happened before. Although U— never complains, I— feels troubled by her composure, a smiling opacity that somehow shuts him out. One day he mentions their father and grows alarmed when no remark, no matter how insensitive, produces any retort. He becomes anxious, starts prowling the apartment, making sure of doors, windows. But as his apprehension increases, his nightly pleasures do too, and with doom approaching, he determines not to flee, recognizing with sinking heart that his fate has outrun him. Finally he awakens one night to the smell of smoke. He calls to his sister, but the crackling of flames is the only reply. The open stairwell and windows, he realizes, will form a chimney, draw the fire toward him. But his strongest feeling is of consummation, of events taking their course. This fragment breaks off unfinished. Its last sentence reads, "As I utter these words the heat of my sister's rage devours the floor beneath my"

In a second fragment, U— and I— go into business. I—'s motivation is unclear, but he decides to make his sister a partner, sharing management and profits equally. However, I—'s reluctance to credit accounts turns out to be his failing, and within weeks U— has taken over. I— withdraws upstairs, venturing into the store less and less often, and finally offers no protest when, during remodeling, U— bricks up every window in their father's facade. I—'s only way out now is through the market.

At this point, U—'s success has restored her confidence, and she's free of her violator's memory at last. But gradually a feeling of uncanniness overtakes her, as if everything has happened before. Although I— never resists her management, she's disturbed by his composure, a silent opacity that somehow shuts her out. One day she locks the upstairs door and becomes alarmed when, after forty-eight hours, he hasn't tried it. She starts listening for his footsteps overhead, monitoring the water bill and electric meter. She fears she's being used, considers liquidating or selling out, but as her apprehension increases, her daily profits do too, and she decides to expand instead, recognizing with a sinking heart that her fate has outrun her. Finally one night she notices all signs of life above have ceased. She creeps up the stairs, calls to her brother, but an echo is the only reply. U— knows that, left to his own devices, I— will have turned upon himself, but her strongest feeling is of consummation, of events taking their course. She enters the apartment, checks every room. I— is not there.

Although the narrator of this fragment is never identified, the final sentence implies that I—'s disappearance, and perhaps the whole novel to this point, has been hallucinated by U—, an incurable schizophrenic confined in a Scottish hospital.

If there exist readers sufficiently persevering to continue to this point, they will have long since abandoned all hope of rewards to come. "Second Story" contains no story, is at best the semblance of a novel, is hardly more than a pun. Its title refers, of course, not to I—'s writing but to I—'s apartment, or more exactly, to the elevation at which he lives "in accordance with my father's will." Its superior perspective ("one flight up") seems essential to I—, but its distance from the fruitfulness in store below unsettles him. For some reason, he confuses coming down to earth with abandoning fiction altogether, as if art's contact with life were somehow corrupting. From first to last I— looks down upon his reader. He never tells us what we want to know.

This condescending reticence is nowhere more apparent than in the unfinished autobiography. There I— finally becomes a novelist, but only by leaving his sister's disinheritance entirely unaccounted for.

The autobiography begins with a promising sentence: "It was always my ambition to meet life face to face, but when I discovered I was my father's heir, I reconciled myself to living at a distance from the ground." Although rich in possibilities, this beginning sentences us to a contradiction that "Second Story" never overcomes. The first story is where nature's produce is stored, but it is also a store in which the products of cultivation are sold. I— insists he loves earth's abundance (calling it "my mother's bounty") and fills pages with ecstasies over "the surprising brightness oranges become," but these effusions appear forced, as if compensating for some lack. Finally, in a lyrically expansive scene, he recognizes the "cornucopia of being" every pumpkin is and throws himself into "the life of a greengrocer," professing bewilderment at that mysterious compulsion he formerly called "literature."

But gradually a feeling of uncanniness overtakes him, as if this devotion to fruitfulness has happened before. Although I—'s customers never haggle, he's disturbed by their composure, a mindless opacity that somehow shuts him out. One day on impulse I— rearranges price tags, valuing kiwis as highly as watermelons, and is alarmed when no one complains. He decides to join a radical party, starts quoting Marx and Bentham, but as his anger increases, his isolation does too, and rather than succumb to desperation, he retreats into the second story, leaving his conclusion up in the air. The produce rots, the store is vandalized, eventually drug dealers move in. I—'s life on earth is over. For the remainder of the book, there's no explanation how I— eats, much less pays his power bill.

(Although the seven journal entries criticize virtually every other aspect of the novel, they never complain about I—'s lack of material support. Noting his apparent indifference to financial motives, the entry for "Day 7" observes that I—'s writing seems increasingly immaterial and remarks on an absence of economy in his narration throughout. However, after deciding that "what's fundamentally the matter here" needs "laying bare," all the journalist ever "lays bare" are twelve *sentences*. Inexplicably, in the editing that follows, the journalist removes every evocative phrase and image quoted in this review.)

If "Second Story" finally does tell a story, it's not the one summarized here, not the narrative of U—'s violation, but the story of I—'s failure to tell that story. U—'s story is a mere pretext. The novel's real subject is the male artist's self-defeat, his narcissistic plea for adoration by the very public he ignores. Nothing ever happens in "Second Story" because its sole aim is to show why nothing *can* happen, why I— can never assume his father's position, how, in the plot against his sister, I— too has been framed.

The autobiography contains a gap, but when it finally resumes, I— has written his novel (entitled, predictably, "Second Story"). Our text provides no excerpts, but an enclosed, unfinished reader's report calls it "a work without prospect of any following," and a jacket blurb (also included) describes it as a *Kunstlerroman* that "records the artist's undoing." Whether I— still lives "at a distance from the ground" is left ambiguous: according to the autobiography, the father's legacy is "a thing of the past," but the blurb says "the author's whereabouts, as of this writing, remain undetermined." Although the autobiography covers ninety pages, there are just two mentions of U—. In an early aside I— complains that she's still working for "that rag" (an unnamed Eastern newspaper), and on the last page of continuous text he contrasts his own amorphous fiction with the plots "to which my sister appears drawn," suggesting that she may be a critic or novelist herself. But I—'s absorption has now become total. How U— escapes her confinement, how she resists the violator of her dreams, no longer comprise his business.

If my synopsis has not sufficiently brought it out, the whole of this tiresome work is further vitiated by an undertone of anti-feminism and indifference to women that many readers will find unsettling. I realize these criticisms are serious, but I do not offer them without reflection. I know nothing of the author's expressed political views, but the qualities I mention (which will strike women readers as obtrusive) are notable precisely because they are unconscious and, I fear, irremediable. The author, like his protagonist I— (there is finally no difference), is afflicted with an obsessive need for abstraction that amounts to little more than fear of the body and love. The whole of his work is permeated by defensive gestures, a kind of embarrassing self-exposure that merely aims to avoid exposure itself. There is something sad about all this. The author is capable of impressive concreteness, as shown by his brief slips into lyricism (for which, of course, the journal entries always repent), but he seems to fear these fleshly pleasures, the invigorating saga of life and mortality. This fear is his sole reason for retreating into narrative indirection and complexities of structure, and most readers—certainly most women readers—will feel it's high time men *stopped doing this*. If the author wishes to encounter life face to face, it's in his power to do so. This is, after all, what novelists have always done.

THE AUTHOR REPLIES:

I know it's always in bad taste to respond to a review, but I don't want to miss this opportunity to thank my sister for her generous remarks on my "Second Story." On all significant points she has recognized my aims and done justice to my work. In writing this novel, I left the story untold, preserving only its insupportable consciousness, precisely as she has explained, and the ineffectuality of my narrator was a transparent ploy to this end. Unlike some reviewers who dismiss what they don't understand, she has been scrupulous in her analysis and shown a rare willingness to withhold judgment until my meaning has made itself plain. As every reader can imagine, the hope of such judiciousness keeps my spirits high.

Her comparison of my book's disintegration with my narrator's discomposure and her comment that, in narrating U—'s suffering, I— tells more than he knows, are further examples of her perceptiveness, but nothing has encouraged me more than her recognition of my unconsciousness of women. Although she may not know this, it has been the major work of my adulthood to liberate myself from the injustices and political repression with which I've been familiar since I was a boy. Having come to maturity during the latest flourishing of women's historic demand for autonomy, I, like so many of my generation, grew to feel feminism in my tissue and bones. A chance sexist remark could send blood to my face. Listening to news-reports I found my heart racing, palms starting to sweat. There seemed no end to the novels I couldn't read with pleasure. In one fashion or another, the consciousness of women constituted the air I breathed, my instincts and terrors, the plots I constantly repeated in my dreams.

As you may imagine, the naturalness of all this at times felt confining. Like my height or bodily imperfections, my discomfort with institutions, laws, policies, friends—virtually everything!—resembled a fate or affliction. Even my attempts at sexist jokes or crude wisecracks were marked by self-consciousness, as if I were merely *faking* machismo, *pretending* to be male. What I felt incapable of was genuine insensitivity, a sincere obliviousness of my own obliviousness. I say this with no pride. I no more chose my dissatisfactions than I chose to speak English. On the contrary, my pride in my indignation, my confidence that anger arose in me from real outrages, from conditions about which people *ought* to feel angry—all this only made my plight more ludicrous. Hadn't every age, even the most brutal, viewed its own anger in just this way? Gradually a feeling of uncanniness overtook me, as if everything I'd grown to know, all my reactions and experience had already happened before.

Perhaps this explains my attachment to the I— I wasn't. Perhaps nothing explains it. I can't tell. But I soon found myself preoccupied with another being. I had no desire to be different. How could I desire what my stomach rose up against? But something about his composure, his faceless opacity, made me feel shut out. I suppose I imagined—or not really imagined, more like imagined imagining, imagined being able to imagine—I imagined myself imagining myself apart from what, in coming to know my sister, I could never not know. There were moments when so much nothing disconcerted me. I tried to overcome it, fearing I— was going nowhere, but because my concentration remained weak, my mind inevitably wandered, leaving me to stare vacantly into space.

I want to make perfectly plain that this other being was inconceivable to me. Perhaps I— wasn't even male. But I knew that his acts were marked by a thoughtlessness unlike any act of mine, an unconsciousness that avoided no consciousness, that denied nothing. After all, to have merely denied what every woman knows, to have pretended ignorance of what no man today can pretend ignorance—why that would be an achievement hardly superior to the Republican party. Wasn't my whole nation in denial of what a woman knows? My task, on the contrary, would be more arduous. I must revert to the nature I naturally avoided, to my uncreated state, must recover an absent-mindedness in which my sister's unaccountability could never be on my account but would be as incalculable as my next heartbeat or every breath escaping me. In short, I— must undo human history.

Of course, I set about the task systematically, discovering one step at a time the impossibility of all that is. I cannot say either of us has made much progress, for progress was the first thing to prove impossible, but I can say his undertaking has completely preoccupied me while composing "Second Story," and although I expect failure will also one day prove impossible, my divided attention has caused me no end of concern. What if, in trying to leave my sister alone, I unwittingly violated her dreams again? Often I've been beside myself with apprehension and would surely have surrendered to fate, had not the continuous prospect of her oblivion prevented me. And so I'm deeply grateful for her reassurance that my work does not contain her, that it betrays no consciousness of any woman, that in it all sensitivity to pain is gone, such that, in withdrawing my interest from her saving's account, my words have finally ceased to be overlooked, coming forth without super vision, occurring to all at one time. Nothing seems harder than to tell what isn't happening, but in reviewing "Second Story," I suspect my sister isn't there.

However, there remains one sentence of her review with which, despite my deep and sincere appreciation, I still must disagree. Personally, I do not see how "Second Story" could have been an excellent novel. This was what attracted me to it. That any man could narrate his sister's disinheritance, tell how he assumed her abuser's place and came to dwell above the market—from the outset, such a plot struck me as fantastic. Only its perpetrator would presume to write it, and only his collaborator could tolerate its being read. The work's conclusion would be the recognition of its own futility, so that its very existence would constitute proof of fraud. Having always known myself as history's fabricator and having never accepted my sister's reality as my own, I seemed the perfect one to undertake it— by which I mean the first story, the one I could never tell. In this way, I lived out the second. My sister's review is entirely correct. I, who write this self-serving epistle, am the impotent and narcissistic I— of the incomplete autobiography, nemesis of novel readers everywhere, undoer of my life's work. Knowing how classic plots were made, I discounted everything in store, leaving my authority groundless. Thus another beside myself was needed to compose my work, for to him alone its words would come as a surprise. And so the I— I wasn't was sentenced without ever imagining what he'd done. As far as I can tell, nothing remotely like "Second Story" has ever been written. For this reason I call it a novel.

pretense

Cleo has always seemed wise beyond her years, for until she turned sixteen she'd never really lived. Or so she recalls. Of course, she'd anticipated her birthday so long by then that clarity now appears hopeless, but still she relives—or tries—that day, its bewilderment of skin, hair, the maddening universe of smells, and finds that each time is the first. So she recalls nothing. She has begun to fear that the world's in reverse, and this possibility casts her into the deepest longing imaginable. For nothing's ever fresh again; the first ache passes unobserved; she sees the crepe myrtle blooming all winter. How many heartbreaks never happened? How many humiliations? She relives each moment to count the times but, mindful of remembering, forgets, is always starting over.

So she stares at the candles, determined to be sixteen just this once, but it's absurd. Her mother's present, this perfume vial, or atomizer really, iridescent, gold-flaked, with its skinny tendril and dangling bulb like a pear—even in her bliss she knows she'll one day think it's godawful—nothing can be experienced only now. Or if it can, Cleo can't—being after all sixteen—care. Her mind's attuned to promises, secrets, the love that's to come.

Which is nothing new. She's grown accustomed to disappointment from her earliest years, even if she never felt it at the time. Cleo once dreamed—"preposterous" is the word—she actually dreamed at ten that she was happy. What she meant, she now knows, wasn't what anything ever means—or if not what it doesn't mean now, then what it won't mean eventually. The frustration, she understands, is built in. To imagine never suffering her own suffering, or knowing happiness wrongly or only afterwards, never while she's happy. It makes her sad. Cleo's maddest wish is to live her life all over again an instant before oblivion. Perhaps then she could finally love and know it.

Can Cleo really know all this at sixteen? "Yes!" she exclaims, pounding her tired old thigh. It is precisely what she knows whenever she recalls! For on her sixteenth birthday the earth gapes, and gazing over this emptiness, this unbridgeable divide, she sees that no change can be quite like it. The point of saffron streetlight cuts her bedspread. She lies perfectly still. And then comes the interminable midnight when the planet starts moving at last.

Afterwards her memory has no room left over. New pastimes may divert her, but she'll never again be deeply surprised. The only mystery remains why she didn't always grasp what she lacked, why, returning, she can't be made to see it even now, or how others can continue to dream that they know too. She resolves the enigma—it is the miracle of her sixteenth year—by undergoing every moment all year long as she'll understand it only sixty years later. The hair of a boy's belly is what she strokes with impossible nostalgia, locked up inside her ancient secret and his childish shuddering skin. If she could, she'd suckle him, cradle her own parents, mother the whole lost world, but cruelest of all, she can already see—even as a seventy-six-year-old woman at sixteen—that countless others have tried and failed.

And so she dies a thousandth time, recognizing the darkness as the secret her mother's present contained. It's the only freedom that never disappoints her, and so enfolding the perfume vial, she becomes—amid bliss and anguish—her freedom's recollection too. Of course, she still knows she can live any part of everything all over, has always already relived it, hasn't ever since her sixteenth year ceased to hope and languish both now and then, has, in short, known her whole story backwards from end to end and so always lived it badly told, requiring ceaseless revision, irreparably botched. But Cleo's tired, despite having just begun to live, and inexplicably happy. She blows out the candles, looks up into her father's smile.

At sixteen she knows better than ever again that no end can be predicted.

mimesis

I know the color blue when I see it, and the flavor of a pear when I taste it; I know an inch when I move my finger through it; a second of time, when I feel it pass; an effort of attention when I make it; a difference between two things when I notice it; but about the inner nature of these facts or what makes them what they are, I can say nothing at all. I cannot impart acquaintance with them to anyone who has not already made it himself. I cannot *describe* them, make a blind man guess what blue is like....

—William James

Why try. Fellow holds his peace long enough til one day well maybe you think he growed accustomed. Telling dont help. Folks believe most anything or some will. But then dying creeps up and so here I go again writing it down dont ask me why. Wrote it once. Words cant never be the same as what it was.

It was back when I was working for mister Eugene Doggitt of Crystal Branch Alabama. Now he was a good one. We had a

goverment contract for surveying spaniards
hell but not all of it. We didnt want none
of that no sir. Not further than the loggers
already drove. We were finding witness trees
and section corners. I was pulling chain.
Now I am thinking I was 21. It was pretty
wild back then.

We used to pass 2 weeks in the swamp.
Sometimes 3. Mister Doggitt would pack in
salt meat. We all carried water. But mostly
we trusted to what we did find. It wasnt
hardly ever bad. Liked rattlesnake meat
best and they was plenty. Folks say they
cant eat it but thats just prejudice.
Tastes sweet. Gator dont taste much. Possums greasy. Coons good too. Fat ones.
Mostly we shot dinner while working. Like I
said it was pretty wild back then. Sometimes we had to hunt. For water you trusted
to springs. Looked for it clear and fast
moving. You feel it cold you know it was a
spring.

This one time it was bad. We wasnt
lost but we was pretty far in. I am thinking they was 4 of us but cant remember only
3. Johnny Hatten what died in the fertil-
izer company fire up in Dothan was the
other one. He was older then me. So how it
came about I dont recall but we got
parched. Johnny and me kept up pulling
chain thinking we would find us a palm to
suck or something until then we all stopped
and started looking in real earnest. Seems
now the swamp wasnt dry but the water
tasted brackish. Or foul maybe. Leastways
we couldnt drink it. I dont know how long
we looked for. Then it got bad. Mister
Doggitt you could see he was worried for
Johnny. So we turned round and started back

but everybody knowed how things was. Man
cant go without water.

Mister Doggitt he says this settlement
Little Sink what aint there now but was
then 4 or 5 houses and a dry goods store
was no more then a days hike. I figured it
was wrong but never said so. We started off
northerly. Inland water runs clear northerly. Just fore midnight we come up on this
what looks like old loggers road or maybe
was made by bear hunters and started following it. Cant make no time in a swamp
after dark. Gators run from a man in day-
light but dont come on one after dark. Then
bout day break we see this sorghum patch
and this colored lady I know later was
Mehetabel and indian not colored but at the
time it was like I say. I remember thinking
she looked old. Not old like my great
grandma more like 60 therebout or thats how
I recollect now. Well we set in to
hollerin. I think Johnny who wasnt saying
much even give a whoop. We figured we was
saved. Sun just nearly bout up. But be
damned she tells us she aint got nothin fit
to drink. I cant recollect how it was but
ground water must of been contamnated I
reckon.

She says a man in a wagon is coming
fore sundown will take us back to town so we
settled down to wait but ever body knows its
bad. Johnny is staring way off like with his
eyes all shiny and his mouth hanging open.
Mister Doggitt looks at me real sad and I
recollect thinking how I am never gone forget that look. Like saying what a sorry mess
and how bad he knowed we was all feeling
when aint nothing any man alive can do. I
didnt say much. It was commencing to scorch.

Now here comes what is the hard part.
Mehetabel she isnt paying us much mind and
I am thinking she has gone off to manure
the sorghum or work this sorry piece of
collard patch right behind where us 3 is
but then I hear her voice or maybe not hear
it exactly. Maybe its like I was sitting
there and start to listen like you do to a
fellow whistling a ways off and your listening without never really listening cause
its not like when your being spoke to. But
then I start to feel different. And I keep
on listening but not really. Like I said
its the hard part. And soon I remember I am
stretched on the ground in this shade and
commencing to get easy and days turning off
right peaceful and then in no time that
wagon is come and we are riding down to the
main road and nearly to this old colored
fellows farm outside Little Sink and Johnny
dont say much but I can tell it aint bad no
more and wasnt till later I recollect how
all hopeless we was feeling and parched.
That was 19 and 33 about.
Now Johnny cant get around for some
days but then he is alright and mister
Doggitt he says we might should wait til
the weather breaks it being so dry and us
needing provisions so we get a ride on a
mail truck far as Meander where the train
comes through. Took me awhile to speak what
I am thinking. Mister Doggitt I seen was
keeping to hisself. I figure Johnny dont
recollect much. So finally I says to mister
Doggitt dont he think how its peculiar. And
mister Doggitt lets on nothing but asks
what do I mean peculiar and I says how I
think something happened with that
Mehetabel whose name we are now knowing and

mister Doggitt he looks at me and I remember my words coming fast and getting all crossed til finally mister Doggitt give out how he must of gone to sleep and that was a end. But I knowed it werent right. They got on the train next day and I am forgetting what reason I give but I stayed. When next mail truck comes I am back to Little Sink.

What it was was listening to Mehetabel I tasted it. Water I mean. I know there werent none but tasting it is later how I recalled.

Folks in Little Sink was friendly enough but still a stranger got to watch hisself. Fore I was there a week though I learn how it aint no secret. It was one afternoon and there was these 4 fellows out front of the general store and this one commences to tell how Mehetabel is near to ruining his wife. Other 3 nods. Has her wanting him to know what it is to birth a baby he says. Tall fellow with half a leg says maybe if shes so all fired anxious to tell folks something she ought to tell his wife bout the war. Which makes the first one laugh. This other one puts in how its hard on women birthing babies. Not nothing a man wants to learn. But then maybe Mehetabel dont know much bout the war half a leg says getting kinda peckish and the first one he pipes up that maybe Mehetabel dont have to know much to tell it and I see ever body nodding at that. So how is that I say and they all turn and look at me. I mean how is that she dont have to know much to tell folks. And this old fellow what aint said nothing says a man cant never know how much he dont know sooner then Mehetabel starts to talking. And then he

commences to tell about this stout Swede
what come down with the railroad. Fellow
what could tote a tie by hisself and he
marries this gal from Pensacola. Its the
old one now talking. I knowed sure as
shooting that gals people hasnt never been
no more then ten mile from anywheres he
says but no sooner then Mehetabel starts in
and bless pat that gal thinks shes born in
Parry France. Other 3 commence to shaking
there heads real solemn. After that I felt
right sorry for that Swede old fellow says.
Man never knowed peace again. He was a mean
cuss though puts in number 4. Thats true
first one agrees but still man has troubles
enough without Mehetabel making more. Half
a leg says she still dont know nothing bout
the war.

So I tell em bout Johnny and me and
the water and I be damned but they aint
even surprised. They nod like aint that
just the way and then turns out they can
tell it all chapter and verse. They commence to explaining how Mehetabel is one of
the Ocheesee what is a indian people lived
south of Little Sink before anything. And
ever one of them was powerful talkers but
of course they never talked English back
then maybe never talked no language a tall
that old fellow says and I see nobody aint
disputing him. Anyway seems Mehetabel what
isnt full blooded has got the gift. And all
4 start in with particulars they has seen
there own self or heard about how she kept
a young fellow quiet two days what had his
arm pulled clean off in a threshing machine
until doctor from over in Limestone come or
else how she made it so Luther Powell this
mean drunk from Natchez couldnt butcher his

own chickens no more for starting to know
what a sorry cuss he looks like coming after em. All manner of such.

It was hard at the time not suspi-
cioning folks was putting me on what with
me being a stranger and all but then I recollected lying underneath that shade tree
by Mehetabel's collard patch and how her
talking at her self worked its way inside
to me and well I cant say I believed every
tale those fellows told but then I dont say
no neither.

While I was in Little Sink I stayed
with this family had some land and a place
to sleep behind the hay barn and needed some
help with the cows. They was a mother and
her boy 9 or 10 and his sister what I think
now couldnt of been no more then 15 and this
old fellow what the mother called Pap and he
was blind. They was a strange lot specially
the children. I learnt pretty early
Mehetabel aint no name a man wants to be
calling on in this house or not around the
mother leastways. So I never brung up what I
am always thinking but one day long about
dusk Pap shows up steering hisself with a
stick and calling out for me. I holler back
and he wonders as how I might like to sit a
spell and watch the sun set. Now nothing
peculiar in that cause I am figuring he is
wanting company and I am the one doing all
the watching. In Little Sink aint much more
to do of a evening.

So he leads us to this spot where they
has built what looks like a deer blind but
aint only a platform bout as high as your
chest and nothing but sawgrass on all sides
so all they is in a salt marsh to see any
man with eyes can see. Theres a split pine

log wide enough for folks to set on. Well
I am getting comfortable when he commence
to say how the sky turns peach pinkish
going southerly to gold this time a year
and violet where the clouds come near the
cypress tops and is it so tonight. Now I
dont say much for a while but then I
allows as how its melon colored but bottoms of the thunder heads is a little
darker. Then he wants to know is it darker
like plums or like persimmons them thunder
heads. I am feeling sort of peculiar now
but I offer as its more like persimmons.
But ripe. Not red I say like you sometimes
see scuppernongs. And soon as I has finished speaking he kind of catches his
breath and grins real broad and settles
back. Its a bleeder he give out. And then
dont say nothing else.

Well hes sure right its a bleeder. Or
I dont mean I ever knowed what a bleeder
was when he said it but fore night I seen
how the darkish color starts to spread not
in patches or little lines or like cobwebs
but more like milk spreads after a bucket
gets kicked only now its not just turning
things wet but like staining everything it
come near so there you are watching and
the clouds and treetops is kind of peculiar and rosey when all of sudden its like
a mans whole skin done give way and his
heart spilt out. Well I am not saying a
word. Maybe I recollect once he asks me is
there a line of purple still left at the
top of those pines north of the sand basin
or later has it started coming out the old
trappers cut but mostly we both is quiet
and I plane forgot he aint seeing what I
am. I cant say how long it lasted.

Anyway making our way back I figure us being acquainted now maybe I could just ask him what I am feeling in a pretty tight place to know. So I beg his pardon and say I am wondering how long it is since he done lost his sight. Well he laughs at that and allows as how he cant rightly say since he dont never recall having none. Now I think he has misheard me and so I ask again but no sir he tells me he come out of his mammy as dark as moonless December. And I just keep walking cause I am pretty sure he has got to know what I am needing to ask next but he dont offer nothing and so after while I beg his pardon again and ask how it is with him never seeing nothing he come to know so much about them sunsets. And he says Mehetabel told me.

Its a spell fore I can get my thinking and his saying to meet up just right. I mean I can feel this big piece of something missing but I aint yet where I can name what it is. Anyhow Pap allows as how what folks in Little Sink know for there own self and what they know cause Mehetabel done told them aint always two things like a fellow might suppose. And then he tells me how back fore folks stopped letting there children listen at her they would all come home talking about mister catfish hunting water fleas underneath the pond lilies or snow stinging your nose on the mountain top or the smell of cegars and ever body just figured it was a ignorant indian talking and never payed much mind. But then one day this boy come home all excited bout fruits what aint never growed in Little Sink and wont eat his mommas pear pie no more and like to pitch a fit bout

how sweet and syrupy them other fruits is
and its pretty quick folks thinking start
to change.

Now you know how sometimes you get a
speck of nothing in your eye and right off
dont more then hardly blink but keep on
doing what your doing just worrying it a
little now and again till fore long its
growed bigger then a bristle hog and aint
no help for it but to stop the whole blamed
world and dig that devil out. Use a Jim
Bowie knife if need. Well thats how I was
commencing to feel standing there listening
to old Pap carry on about younguns
imaginings. I kept quiet long as he talked
but no sooner then he quits its like I cant
stand it. But that aint no more then just
notions I figure I must of shouted at him.
Already I am thinking it aint what I mean
to say.

Old Pap looks surprised. For a minute
he dont say nothing. Then he turns them
wobbly eyes of his up at me and asks hasnt
I noted that girl. And no use acting like I
dont know what he means. Its her I said
already was 15 and am telling you now folks
called Forsythia. And Pap is meaning how
she dont never laugh nor do whats regular
for a girl but just is wandering round the
barnyard all day and humming somewhat and
acting afar off. I allowed as I had noted
it. Cant no body tell how Mehetabel done it
Pap says nor what it is exactly for a child
to know but Mehetabel done told her and now
that girl knows she is born to die.

I was 21 back then and a fool. Even
fellow blind as Pap could of told that
child was peculiar but werent no mount of
peculiar could scare me away. Fore I was

round that place a week I was up to nonsense with her and by the time Pap had his
say I had seen enough to know he wasnt just
fibbing. Danged unsettlingest creature I
ever met. I seen her one morning standing
in her mommas sunflowers and I come up all
pleasant like and spoke some foolishness
and she just peers up at me for such a
spell I commence to suspicion she is simple
but then she smiles this smile what is
hardly big enough to say is a smile but
soothed me all the same and says kindness
is a blessing and how she is grateful for
it. Well I dont say nothing to that. Her
voice dont sound like no girls voice nor
like no ladys neither but is real quiet and
steady without hardly a quiver or no live-
liness and I reckon one a us needs to keep
on talking but she dont give no sign its
gone be her so I am hunting up some smart
remark but aint finding airy a word till
fore long I am just standing there like I
am simple too. We look at each other then
and she dont so much as blink a eye and I
dont mind telling you I started to feel
plum scared. Like as if one of us dont commence to talking soon we gone be there till
doomsday.

Well I got outer there some ways but
aint no time til I start waking up at night
thinking bout her. I would hear that voice
and get to worrying bout her laying right
there in that house not 50 feet further
then I was laying and it like to start my
legs to bouncing. Being scared just made it
worse. I told you I was a fool. Anyway soon
as old Pap done said that bout her and
Mehetabel you can believe I got curiouser.
I asked him how folks come to learn of it

and he recollects back when she was a
little thing how she kept after Mehetabel
to tell her bout heaven where her momma
done said her daddy was living and her
momma never seen much harm in that. But
then one afternoon she aint home at
suppertime and when she turns up real late
her steps on the porch is heavy like a body
whats drunk. Pap allows as how his daughter
as I told you was momma to Forsythia never
done told him all of it but he was there
when the child come home and heard her
talking bout her daddy werent gone to
heaven after all. It was her words. My
daddy aint just nothing now. Seems that
happened 6 years or better fore the time I
am now telling about and Pap said the child
aint been regular since.

    You might of think after hearing so
much queer talk I am bout to tell you I
done forgot that Mehetabel business and
high taled it home but you can think again.
Part of it was getting a taste of something
what if you dont drink your fill of it aint
never gone give you no peace and part of it
was that gals voice. I recollect now as how
it sounded old not like Pap was old but old
like cypress knees and then fresh as a
tiger lily too. Anyways werent no use in
trying to forget it. So all I can think of
soon as Pap done finished is how now I got
me that smart remark I was needing before
to keep talking to that Forsythia. And sure
enough wasnt no more then the next day I
find her lolly gagging underneath this big
laurel oak what is still standing behind
the Holiness church in Altha and I walked
over real quiet though I can see she werent
doing nothing and she dont look up for a

minute and then she do but slow and easy
like she werent a little surprised and give
that smile what aint hardly a smile and I
offers as me and her grandaddy done seen
the sun go down the other night. Well
durned if she dont say she never seen it
till then neither. It takes me a minute
fore I can straighten out how what I am
meaning is its peculiar seeing a sunset
with a blind man and what she is meaning is
peculiar some other way. But starting over
dont help. Her eyes commence to stare off
and I thinks uh oh doomsday coming again
and so I offers as how its real good we
both done seen that same sky. And thank you
Jesus that starts her talking. Tells me how
she never knowed it were flat what with its
innards all outside and the purple not just
on things underbelly but plum through so as
ever thing for a body to see is right there
waiting. Well that was a tight place. I am
commencing to feel scared but I says to my
self no sir you gone too far to turn a yellow coward now. So I nod and allow how I
would like to see it like she has said too.
And be durned if morning dont break out in
that girls face. She grabs holt of my hand
and next I know she done dragged me off.

And that was how I come to witness
Mehetabels talking for my own self. Or
tried. I dont mean as to how I hadnt witness
it before cause I suppose some folks call
witnessing what happened there to me and
Johnny Hatten and mister Doggit beside that
collard patch but I never recollected it as
witnessing but only as something come over
me. Like I said its the hard part. Anyhow I
follow that girl up to this cabin which I am
knowing later is where Mehetabel lives with

her pack a worthless dogs what is too shiftless to even lift a head at you but the
cabin is nice with windows and a new tin
roof. I dont go up to the porch cause I am
still a might uneasy but that girl do and
pretty soon Mehetabel come out and they
commence to talking as regular as you
please. Aint neither one saying no more then
just what ever body says. Bout the seasons
changing and swamp fixing to come up. Anyhow
I remember Mehetabel telling how the rain
that morning brung the smell of jasmine
through her window strong enough to stir the
taters and that girl listening at her real
close and then well I dont recollect nothing
else. Not Mehetabels talking no ways. Makes
a fellow want to give up this writing business for good. One minute I am making sure
not to miss a word and hearing nothing to
mention and then next minute I am noting this
freshness what come off a myrtle bush when a
fellow shakes it and smells like new cut pine
only dryer and seeing not more then 6 inches
from my face this little milk colored flower
what cant be no different from them I been
seeing my whole life but has a raggedy edge
on one side with a yellow line snaking between its 2 halfs and over at the end a 4
corner patch of black rods with this long
dangly

     I am stopping right there fore you are
thinking I has gone crazy too. But that
flower was its own self and I dont mind
saying so. Anyhow I figure I must of studied it more then a hour cause when I look
up that girl is gone and the sky is dark
and there I am still standing not 40 feet
from Mehetabels cabin and aint nothing but
a lamp burning inside and the woods is as

quiet as I dont believe they has ever been since. I will leave out about getting back home that night but next day when I seen that girl I mean to say she come right up to me like your favorite coon dog and dont speak nor nothing but just stand there staring off and not giving a sign she is ever fixing to say boo nor leave neither and I think now that I am telling it that what must of scared me more then even what scared me before was there I was standing next to that gal and staring off and saying nothing and not feeling scared a tall.

I am living in Little Sink better then 5 months.

No man cant tell whats in his heart leastways not without it surprising him. After all the strangeness I been through I felt right uneasy and wasnt long fore I started to thinking. Not when that Forsythia was round. Could of stood to do a sight more thinking then. But when I was by my own self I started to thinking maybe what with Pap and them sunsets and me and Johnny Hatten and seeing Mehetabel and that girl talking how I couldnt never just go back to living regular again. Not like I up and said as much but you understand it was worrying me. What if I was to turn as peculiar as that boy stopped eating his mommas pear pie or that fellow couldnt butcher his chickens. Well you can believe I wanted to get to the bottom of that Ocheesee business then. So I come up with a plan. I think since that Forsythia is now more then anything else twixt me and the regular way I was always being if I could just fix it up so she were back regular too it would make a end of ever thing. You are likely think I

was a bigger fool then I has allowed and I
aint disputing it. But seemed to me at the
time as how folks in Little Sink werent no
more then ordinary but under this kinder
spell or something and if a man was only to
say the right word or give them a shake
they would go back to acting natural as you
please. I am now supposing it was all wrong
but didnt seem wrong then especially that
part bout folks being ordinary.

So I try to tell that girl how what
Mehetabel told her aint no more then just
words and it is real sad and all bout her
daddy but Mehetabel dont know no more then
her momma nor her own self where her daddy
done gone and dont mean her daddy aint in
heaven or some wheres but only how folks
aint got no business going on about what a
body cant know. And a whole lot more. But
danged if she aint got the first notion
what I am saying. She says she dont recollect Mehetabel talking bout her daddy nor
heaven nor her own self ever thinking more
then what she is thinking at that minute
which dont seem like much. Leastways she
cant tell me none of it. Bless me if I aint
even sure that girl knows what words like
dying and heaven means. Well I keep at her
a while but aint long fore she is staring
off to doomsday again and I has to give it
up. She smiles that itty bitty smile then
and things start to turn rosey and fore I
know it I has clean forgot bout that plan.
I see then how it aint no use talking to
her. Talking is all whats the matter in the
first place.

That should of been my first warning
but werent. Seems like it wasnt no time
fore I am figuring how if I cant wake up

folks in Little Sink that aint cause they
aint under no spell but is cause only her
what has made them that way knows the words
to use. So I decided to pay a visit to
Mehetabel. Now I dont mind telling you it
werent nothing I was hankering to do. I
mean I done felt for my own self how her
talking makes a man forget ever thing and
what am I gone do I wonder if she commence
to cast a spell on me. Fellow might not
even know. But soon as I would get to worrying I would recollect that Forsythia
smiling and werent no help for me but to
keep my thinking on a short rein and stay
outer my own way. So I follows that path
she done showed me and come up on that
little cabin where is those shiftless dogs
lying on the porch but aint no body home.
Which was kinder a relief. Leastways until
I turn round and see coming down the path
this body bent double neath a gunny sack.

Now I knowed Mehetabel was just a old
indian lady what lived alone and didnt have
folks to do for her but I aint somehow been
thinking bout her toting groceries. So I am
just standing there and she is getting
closer and she looks up and I look back and
we still aint so much as said howdy when
she give out this long sigh and allows how
its a marvel. I say whats a marvel. And she
says bout how babies where I come from
is born without mommas. And I says my momma
was a Bascom from Vidalia. And she says she
dont know bout that but she knows cant be
no womans son will stand there while a old
lady breaks her back. Well that gets me to
moving. I help her off with that gunny sack
and ease it down in the pantry and still
them dogs aint so much as fidgit and after

we has sit and fanned a spell I work round
to what I come to say. Well sir she listens
at ever thing bout how that girls heart is
broke what with her daddy passing and her
thinking dying aint more then just nothing
and how it would be a sight better if
Mehetabel told her aint no knowing bout
heaven or such so she could get back to
being a girl again and a mess of other
stuff I cant recollect now. Well when I
finish I am near outer breath but I can see
something aint right. Mehetabel is sitting
there with her mouth hanging open saying
nary a word. So I thinks maybe they is
something she dont understand and am fixing
to start over when she give her head a
shake and lets out this whistle. Boy she
says you gone plum crazy.

Now I aint ready for that. It takes me
a minute to figure how she means she aint
never done with that Forsythia more then
just act friendly to a child whats lonesome
since her daddy died. She dont let on to
knowing no more bout heaven nor what dying
is then that Forsythia let on to knowing
when I asked her before and I aint sure as
how I just believe her but cant see nothing
in how she is acting thats like a old
indian putting a fellow on neither. Well
seems like more was said. I remember some
business bout that gal what think she come
from Parry France. But nothing is getting
us no closer so finally I up and asks
Mehetabel to talk to that Forsythia for me.

And what you want said she says.

What ever gone straighten out that
confoundedness keeps her from acting regular I says.

Bout dying and all she says.

And at first I aint sure what to answer but then I say not just bout dying but bout how aint nothing in living what wont let a body get past it. Aint right I say for a girl to be never talking or just standing there all the time thinking how folks is all gone leave and nothing plea- surable lasts when ever body knows there is more suns to be setting then just this one.

And Mehetabel looks up real serious and asks is it a fact.

Is what a fact I say back.

Bout them suns.

How it aint more then just this one I ask.

And she give a nod.

And so I say hasnt she heard folks say sure as the sun gone rise tomorrow and such.

And she allows she has heard it.

Well then I say.

And Mehetabel done sit there the long- est time not moving and with this deep look like she is weighing ever word. Then she hauls her self up and says in a tired way. Aint no helping you boy. You in love.

Well its alot later I learn from Pap how the reason Mehetabel aint admitting ever thing is cause when she wasnt hardly more then a girl her own self she done talked her way out of a husband and she is likely not wanting to do the same for that Forsythia. He told me as how this fellow Zedekiah folks called Zed took a fancy to Mehetabel but she scared him off talking bout the mischief come of him marrying a indian. They was heaps of folks but mostly women blamed her for it since aint no way to catch a husband telling him the badness

first. But Pap reckoned as how maybe
Mehetabel hoped Zed would stay on
irregardless. Werent in him though. Any way
it was later Pap told me it and seemed at
the time how that explained alot. I mean
werent like Mehetabel could of talked up
heaven and Parry France and drinking water
then soon as I asked her plum forgot.

Now its getting on toward fall and I
am knowing folks in Little Sink better and
still working a little for that girls momma
and helping ever body out with there har-
vesting and even triangulating a field or 2
best I could without regular chains or
transit and near bout ever minute I aint
working I am hanging round that Forsythia.
It is a peculiar way to be. Seems now we
never did nothing more then just stand all
close and stare off at what later I couldnt
much remember. Sometimes I ask myself has I
gone clean out of my head. But a fellow can
keep his thinking in one direction and
travel a pretty far distance in the other
fore he ever wonders is that stranger there
off yonder his self. Anyways by now I
knowed Mehetabel aint gone say no words for
me what will wake that girl and aint much
hope of her turning regular no ways else.
So I think and I think but it is a long
time fore I hit on what to do next.

You wouldnt guess it now but I was
once not much in the writing way. I could
print my letters alright and cipher but
back then werent much use for handwriting
proper. What folks call curse it. Man did
his business face to face. Why I seen
cattle farms bought and sold and never more
then a nod and a shake but thats another
story. Anyway one day I am in the dry goods

store and I come across a box full of them
yellow pencils like mister Doggitt
scribbled down figures with. It give me a
idea. Well I bought 2 and ordered a hard
back tablet what took 3 weeks to come but
then I had ever thing and commenced to
work. It was hard going. I would spend all
morning back of that barn making words what
had there letters strung together like
washed shirts on a line. Werent that much
to hooking up a m or a l. Just loops an
such. But that b or q didnt give a man much
quarter. I took to practicing writing what
folks said not ever word you understand but
enough. So I could recollect later. Had a
few letters what done the work of 4 or 5
and breviations. It seemed a queer way to
do never lifting up your pencil. Like swimming with your head down. But real fast.
After while I got so I was writing quick as
a city feller talked. Nearly.

So one afternoon I am out front of the
sundries and this shorty name of Rob Robbin
Robber cant recollect now but folks called
him JT. Well he is full of this bad turn a
chicken farmer done him and this other boy
name of Clarence what was a chicken farmer
his self keeps putting in how chickens is
particular and fellers what dont know bout
it best not talk. Rest of us got our work
cut out just trying to keep clear. Seems
they was me and a couple more.

Anyways that shorty JT turns his self
up a notch saying how the man what thinks
JT Rob Robby Roberts somewhat dont know
nothing bout chickens better not say it out
loud and that Clarence holler back how
maybe he aint saying so but maybe he aint
not saying so neither. Which commences that

JT to swearing. Seems aint gone be no end
to them 2 making folks uncomfortable and
the rest of us is getting hopeful of a
earth quake or something when outer no
place Mehetabel come up. Sounds peculiar
but werent. Anyway JT is damning and
hellfiring and Mehetabel just crooks her
head and wonders does any body recollect
how thunder heads is at night specially
when a fellers little and watches ever
thing outer his window and some times you
can tell they is clouds but other times
your just seeing stars wink and so know
between you and ever thing they is this
bigness blowing so its really all your
seeing whenever folks ask what your seeing
but you dont say your seeing thunder heads
you just say sky.

Dont no body move. Even that shorty JT
aint hardly mumbling. Me I edge off to one
side and get out my writing tools.

Now if I had of kept that tablet I
could tell you today ever word exactly like
Mehetabel spoke it but as you will hear I
aint got it no more and what is besides that
were the only time nothing happened when
Mehetabel spoke so really werent much to
forget nohow. Well she kept going on bout
being 8 or 9 and your feet slapping the dirt
then hopping right back up again each time
you run and the air passing under your arms
and how your body aint no bigger then a
acorn hardly so that sometimes you get a
good speed up you aint sure but at the edge
of things maybe you will just lift off. And
more bout lightenings and magnolia leaves
and the smell of cornstalks in a drought. I
recall a sight better now then I thought but
still they is alot I am forgetting.

So I am stringing my ts and ws together thinking how later I can point at the
words caused all the mischief and show that
Forsythia how Mehetabel done it when bless
me if I dont look up and see them other
fellows gawking in the peculiarest way. Even
that ornery JT. I mean there eyes is big and
there jaws is hanging open like they is
seeing right through whats in front of them.
Now here comes the hard part. I am real
quick starting back to write so as not to
miss a word when real gradual I feel my loop
dee loops getting harder to make and my hand
commencing to stiff up and that pencil stopping and there I am just listening like any
body and well right then I knowed it aint no
spell folks has been under. No sir. It is
just a old half indian woman going on bout
the smell of sassafras tree root and spring
water on your ankle and the way a deer will
stand and look you in the eye or the sound a
branch makes snapping in the woods like this
world is a big place full of no man cant
tell what and your alone in it for feels
like a long time then feels like a short
one. Like I says its coming back. But no
matter cause its only Mehetabel talking now
not some magic lady and she aint saying more
then what anybody aint born witless cant
know and here these fellows is all big eyed
and hang jawed like they never heard such.
It plum made me sick. Well right then I put
down that tablet and left it setting beside
that store where I reckon some stranger
found it and couldnt make head nor tale of
all them breviations.

After that wasnt nothing ever the
same in Little Sink. Leastways not for me.
Folks overnight stopped being ordinary and

commence to seem plum loco. Couldnt hardly
stand to be round them. Even that mother of
Forsythia what got in such a dither bout
Mehetabel ruining her children. I felt like
hollering at her hell aint no more then
just jabber. But by then I knowed it werent
no use. If theres one thing I feel bad
about its that girl. I should of been man
enough to tell her I was going but werent
no way to explain. I mean feller couldnt
live regular round folks like that and that
girl werent gone be different no wheres
else. All the same I should of told her.
She probably wouldnt of payed no mind. Just
stared off.

Anyhow soon as I was packed which
werent hardly a minute since when I come to
Little Sink I didnt have no more then I
could tote and all I added since was them
pencils I went looking for old Pap. I found
him in a pecan grove standing by hisself
with his head tilt back and them wobbly
eyes open like if it were a seeing fellow
you would of said he was studying the
weather. Well I commence to tell him good
by and he dont let on to hear. Just keeps
his head tilt back and I suspicion hes
bitter bout that girl but then he asks me
is the sky turn fall blue yet. Well I know
it were wrong but something bout him asking
me that brung up a hardness in my chest and
I answer back what does that matter to a
old blind man.

Now Pap he seems kinder surprised at
that. He give me this look what werent no
look I can describe cause of his eyes going
ever which a way and says how it matters
cause fall blue is more peaceful then
summer blue like any body can tell you.

I cant explain it but them words were gasoline on a grass fire. Like I done been preached at by one of them talking magpies I seen at the farm show in Albany what dont know more then this here typing machine what it says. So I stick my jaw out and asks is that a fact and he allows how it is and I say well him being such a expert may be he can help me.

He perks up at that.

Aint no secret that sky is blue I say and I reckon ever body knows that ocean is the same. And of course no man cant see no ocean in Little Sink even if he got 4 eyes in his head but Pap give a nod. And I reckon we both know how that

And here I felt kinder queer but gone on.

how that Forsythias eyes is blue too. And he nods again but dont give out like neither of us is thinking nothing bout it. Well I figure its easy telling folks bout that sky and all I say. But hows a feller gone tell folks bout them eyes.

Now he give a queer little laugh and allows it aint no easy task and just how am I meaning to do it. But I am ready for that and say right back how I has asked his help and is he gone begrudge me. Well he give out that laugh again then dont say nothing for a minute and I am feeling pretty smart and figuring he is gone cry uncle when he asks do I recall in July a hour before sun up when the air feels so near to cool a good sneeze like to scare it off.

And I say so.

Well he says you know how if you walk out then and set on the porch never rocking

and the cypress trees are stillest they
gone get and yonder by the barn the wrens
starting up that teakettle teakettle and
you smell whats nearly one whiff of jasmine but your feeling so fresh you aint
sure it aint just imagining and there like
that not hardly breathing you think aint
nothing gone change.

Well he stops and I wait a minute and
then I see its a question. So I say yep I
know bout it not sure I do but not wanting
to sound ignorant neither.

And Pap give his head a nod and said
well sir its what the blue of that sky is
like. And he dont wait a instant to argue
or nothing but pitches in bout how during a
long dry time in the middle of the heat
under a grandaddy oak what has branches
grow out wider then tall and bent back down
to the ground on all sides so when the sky
gets dark and a storm come up and rain as
bigger then a mans fist is splattering the
dirt and thunders coming through your feet
and lightening sparking in them branches
its just like something down under you has
climb up inside you and your wanting to run
but aint no getting loose and you might
just feel plum terrorfied if you werent
wild happy and come to think of it you dont
know what you are.

And he paused again and I seed I was
to answer and so must of said something
cause he done smile and says its like them
blue eyes.

Now Pap is finished talking and for a
minute neither of us says nothing. It felt
peculiar. I mean aint more then a lot of
nonsense anybody could of spoke but not
just ever day you hear a feller speak it.

Its another of them hard parts I reckon. Anyways I am standing there trying to recollect myself and watching Paps eyes swimming round in his head when I starts to feel like it has happen again. I been bewitched. Aint sure how nothing is or where I am in the middle of it and cant hardly remember its only blind Pap there in front of me. So I heft my sack real quick and give out a laugh and say that bout rising early and getting rained on and such aint more then just words. Blue is something else.

And old Pap he dont miss a lick. He just looks kinder puzzled and asks what is that.

What is what I say.

Something else he says back.

And I point at that sky and say its that right there.

What he asks again.

And I must of been getting pretty hot cause I remember my voice were loud. It kinder embarrassed me. Blue I say.

Blue he says.

I am pointing at it I holler.

And he dont say nothing then and I am commencing to feel bad for acting all rude to a poor creature what never done me no bad turn. What cause I got. But feller with a idea in his head is like a locomotive on a downhill track. So I tell Pap how all I was ever meaning was how blue is what folks are seeing when they point at that sky and aint no telling a body what cant see what its like but folks as can see know.

Blue he says real soft.

And I says thats all the something else I ever meant.

And he looks real thoughtful a minute
and then he says I see.

Happened just like that. As natural as
you please. I see. Well it were the end of
talking. Never even said good by. Last I
recollect he were still standing in that
pecan grove his head tilt back and wobbly
eyes open for all the world just like you
or me or any body.

I never set foot in Little Sink again
and I come to decide that Mehetabel werent
likely much different from moving pictures
or tv. May be if ever thing what happened
happened over wouldnt none of it happen the
same. But some times I get to thinking bout
that Johnny Hatten business and I dont
know. I mean we was goners. Parched throat
cant drink only words. Done told myself it
were dreaming but cant forget. And then you
what hasnt never seed that Forsythia commence to reading bout them eyes just like
you knowed too. And them sunsets and pear
pie and smell of myrtle and ever thing.
There it goes getting all mixed up again.

Like I said. Writing dont help.

'bus

I got on a bus, the one I'd missed before. I'd taken it to my mother's house, the cleaners and school, most famously to meet my sister, who can be as hard to locate as God. I'd carried books and burdens and sometimes messages. Usually I was young, crazy, broke, either black or white, occasionally cool but never rich. For reasons I can't explain, whenever I've taken the bus to straighten bedclothes or iron shirts, I've always been her, never me, as if some bus rides necessitate others. Who knows where it stops? One thing for certain: when I've gotten on a bus, I've been in a city. You board Greyhounds, take the subway, fly Delta, but buses can only be gotten on where humans go in droves, live on top of each other. Wherever there are buses, there must be crowds.

I got on a bus and found it empty. Of course, there was a driver. If you say, There was nobody on the bus, or, I had the bus to myself, or as now, The bus was empty, nobody thinks spirits were driving. (Bus ride of the Ancient Mariner.) At a play rehearsal, you can notice that the theater is empty. Sometimes people leave a party because there's nobody there. When the housekeeper answers your knock, if her employer's away, she may say, Nobody's home. Nobody doesn't mean no body. An empty bus means plastic seats, metal poles, signs, dry mud, rubber mats, oxygen, a change machine, string, bell, housefly, countless micro-organisms, me and—don't be silly—a driver. Empty space is empty like that. Empty fields are empty like that. Columbus discovered that kind of uninhabited land.

But the bus was also empty in the way only buses can be empty. Every new world is empty because we who are us haven't discovered ourselves in it yet. A house can be empty the way a body can be, because no one's ever really at home inside. There are as many ways a theater can be empty as ways a theater can be full. Some of these ways resemble buses. In an empty bus, a crowd is missing. What's missing is a crowd's noise and deliberate silence. The teenage lovers and the overflowing woman are missing. Your shame's missing. Romance is missing. The odor of skin is missing. But missing most of all is a bus-crowd's principal achievement, privacy while belly to butt with strangers. Which can be missing in fiction, in fact, so palpably that when I'm actually sitting here, my muscles and heart and lungs notice it before I do. I slouch, I spread, I sprawl. I breathe so easily I don't breathe. Goggle-eyes, rubber-neck. Bus is beginning to happen.

The empty bus transported me here. Unlike any bus I've ever gotten on before, the empty bus moves like every bus I've ever gotten on before. Sluglike, it makes its way. Fords cross over, cycles stop, someone following the law beats his horn. The empty bus knows nothing. Accumulating momentum with time, it conceives its terminal, an unforeseen point, so that requesting stops becomes a presumption. When you pull the cord on a crowded bus, you never go naked. Others defy fate alongside you, new rebellions hide past ones, but an empty bus bares your designs. What makes humans dream that enormous structures will convey them? No matter. My heart beat faster, my stomach tensed, I strained to see up ahead, when suddenly, the driver started to ignore me.

Crowds ignore nobody. If the grandmother beside the window speaks to the surly youth across the aisle, she doesn't ignore her seatmate or the off-duty cop beside them or anyone else she doesn't speak to. No passenger not involved gets excluded. Everybody has no body. But inside an empty bus, privacy turns peculiar. For instance, I wasn't so sure the driver and I weren't traveling together. If I'd stood to pull the cord, I might have said, Excuse me or Rough weather Thursday or just Bye. I know it's a faux pas, but I don't know the reason. Drivers talk. I've seen them, usually after dark, with a passenger sitting sideways in the front seat, hanging from the pole. They have a kind of frankness. It's done without eyes. Their token is a cheekbone, turned just slightly or, if the passenger's in back, the left ear. At a pitch of enthusiasm, they give you half their face—but eyes always on the road. The art requires insinuation, like they'd look at you if they weren't looking ahead, which, of course, you want them to do. So maybe the driver of the empty bus wasn't unaware of me, maybe I'd just noticed what he wasn't doing. After all, was I after conversation? After what then? All the same, I felt uneasy. The empty bus had me in it, and the driver was a stranger.

In stories I've gotten on buses to go where stories happen, and I've stared out bus-windows at the places in stories where they don't, and sometimes I've witnessed riders do what happens only where stories do, shriek, Mother! Darling, sweetheart, wait! The bus stops for a glimpse of mayhem. Everyone exits. In the end we know where we are. But riding in the empty bus, I kept losing my place. Every route is supposed to be terminal, but between me and my destination, I couldn't determine a distance, as if the journey were pointless—not like a joke but like an imaginary number. I couldn't plot it. Wherever I located me, the intervening stops seemed unlimited and progress unaccountable. Maybe an empty bus—unlike trains, ships, carriages, stages—just isn't a vehicle for fiction. For you can start a train of events or climb on board one, and ships, if hard, improve a fellow, so that upright men, no matter how poor their carriage, may be borne to good fortune in the end, the moral being that every stage of our journey will be one day passed through. But if a bus is empty, all you can do is *get on*. Like a bandwagon. The event is just a step up, slightly forward, toward the center, so what's achieved is a surface, like the earth's, where you find yourself among strangers, moving. Depending means hanging on. It's not at all clear this container is mine.

And yet, if not for me, would it be at all? A time will be when it won't. Buses go with petroleum, demographics, miasma, wrist-watches. When the world is empty, no body's going to miss them, but the person who considers buses a convenience is forgetting what words mean. Once upon a time, we mounted horses. For no obvious reason, these creatures allowed us on their backs. A horse is a being. It weighs a thousand pounds, can be wider than an oil drum, possesses mild affections but astonishing force. The person who says horses had no choice hasn't been thrown. Horses won't live in a garage, don't tolerate being treated like toasters. How could what conveys us be immaterial? There's a sound that's the sound of a bus, a smell that's the smell of a bus, a sign that's the sign of a bus, a stop that's the stop for a bus, a bus lane, a bus hangar, a bus depot, a camaraderie from sharing a bus, a conversation as long as a bus ride, an uneasiness standing too near one, an agitation you feel waiting for one, an isolation at being late—yet again—because your bus is, and a peculiar kind of elation, brief but sharp, anonymously ours, that takes voice like, Here comes the bus! Outside the empty bus, is the land inhabited? Will a body feel at home there? How can humans be located?

I got on the empty bus and found all waiting. Enormous vehicles had transported me before, but I'd only passed through them. Now I was here. The footing felt dubious, so that, if the bus hadn't literally been empty, I might've fallen for anything, but the more crowded the container became, the more every body hung together and, for the duration of a ride, the arrangement held up. We felt the earth tremble, heard a roar—horns, brakes, oaths—and, blind but determined, we made our way. I laughed my head off. As contrivances go, of course, it was pretty pointless. Who could say where the contraption might leave us? But what made this fellowship matter was, regardless of the momentum we accumulated, we never got ahead of ourselves. I was crammed in between these teenage lovers and an overflowing woman—a housefly buzzing my ear, clumps of dried mud disintegrating under my feet—when I pushed up against the window and, instead of seeing the untold world, I saw my nose, here in the midst of all. It felt weird, like an empty bus. We rode and we rode and we rode. I struck up a conversation with Frank, the driver. After a while I asked, Hey, where does this thing stop?

Omnibus in boldface slash accent mark aye with two dots em en schwa space bee schwa ess slash lower-case en italicized parenthesis eff are period uppercase ell all parenthesis large number one in boldface a public vehicle usually automotive and four-wheeled and designed to carry a comparatively large number of passengers parenthesis on Mile End Road from the top of an omnibus in boldface which paused at the end of a dingy street lighted by only occasional flares of gas we saw two huge masses of ill-clad people clamoring around two hucksters apostrophe carts from which the auctioneers scornfully flung decaying vegetables dash Jane Addams parenthesis or commonly bus.

torture!

Among the novels I'll never write is one about the American anthropologist, B. R. Rymer, who during the forties became concerned about the ramshackle state of moral knowledge. He believed no practice was more distinctively human than cruelty, but until his time, its study had been hampered by provincialism. In the aftermath of the war and perhaps in response to revelations about the death camps, Rymer committed himself to an exhaustive study of torture, one that, he hoped, would provide data for a more systematic approach to atrocities in the future.

I imagine him writing his "1949 Preface" before beginning his field research. The crucial section is the third where he argues that all past studies of torture have been "disguised polemics" against it. These studies gathered data—"to the extent they gathered data at all"—only as evidence in a "case." As a result, no one seriously committed to knowledge has been able to profit from their findings. Still more distressing, the many individuals devoted to humanitarian goals—"who, though not scientists, deserve unqualified respect for accomplishments in other fields"—have lacked the information necessary for intelligent decisions.

"If there is to be moral activity," he says, "it must be based not on prejudice but on facts," facts that have been acquired "as nearly as possible...without moral bias." A crux is this sentence: "Recent events should make excruciatingly clear that action based on unsound beliefs is far more dangerous than inactivity or indifference."

Near the end of February 1950, Rymer completed his preliminary studies and sailed from San Francisco. For several years he crossed and recrossed the planet recording horrors. I see this as a period of struggle. His first task must be to train himself. It proves difficult. Scientific aims have to be explained to persons oblivious of science. In some cases he must spend months convincing corrupt officials of his trustworthiness, and once he gains admittance to an interrogation by sharing technical information. Knowledge can't be partisan, he realizes, and efficient torture is actually more humane. He's not surprised to learn that torturers are often ignorant of physiology, neurological tolerances, etc. They regularly kill victims or produce unconsciousness just when results seem promising. Rymer learns to employ his expertise to advantage, improving his own relations with his subjects and often curtailing a victim's pain measurably. This last brings him satisfaction, but he doesn't let himself become confused about it.

The plot divides here. If I follow a phrase in an early letter—"local officials as brutish as their archaic methods" (June 13, 1952; Windemeer lib.)—the story takes a political turn. During the first four years Rymer concentrates on legal torture and studies criminal torture only if opportunity affords. But to his surprise, the criminals prove more illuminating. Legal torturers are usually untrained policemen or poorly educated military conscripts from the agricultural districts, while criminals are disciplined, often with years of experience. He hypothesizes that a promising field might be among criminals who work to high-minded ends, that is, freedom fighters, liberation armies, and terrorists. However, Rymer has no success observing these experts. Despite palaver about enlightenment and the future, progressive torturers care less for science than Rymer has imagined, and their distrust of strangers is unequaled, even by thugs. Rymer tries bribery, diplomatic influence, letters from famous anarchists. Nothing helps. Then one night, happening to be present at the capture of a spy, Rymer takes a hand in torture himself. He feels morally revolted, of course, but if not for sacrifices, how does civilization advance? The terrorists are amazed. Never have they witnessed this art. All suspicion vanishes, and with their cooperation, Rymer achieves his most significant results.

The alternative version turns on Rymer's prodigious writing.[1] Initially Rymer restricts his record-keeping to quantitative data and categorical descriptions. His hostility to anthropology as "high-brow travelogue" is, of course, notorious. However, sometime during the first year he starts the journal, primarily as a record of oddities but also for personal notes. I imagine him devoting more and more time to these notes and calling them his "outlet." (His troublesome self-fascination doesn't appear in the journals until much later.) He soon recognizes that he has underestimated his project. Much of his adult life will be required for torture, and instead of a single volume, he now knows he's creating—if time and health permit—a library. His journal entries become chapter drafts, which he revises, and because they exist in versions, he carries them all in a suitcase. The suitcase arouses curiosity. Again and again he shows its contents to smugglers, colonels, chieftains, and for no clear reason, the abundance of pages raises him in everyone's respect. The torturers insist his book will become a movie. Nothing Rymer says will shake this conviction, and because their admiration facilitates his work, he plays along.

In this second version, the suitcase becomes the cause of the terrorists' suspicion in the first version. Inexplicably, the pages that increase a police sergeant's esteem foreshadow double-cross to a revolutionary. Only traitors, the guerillas tell him, revise their story. I'm unclear how the suitcase connects with Rymer's participation in torture, but in this

---

[1] The University of Wisconsin "Collected Papers" project has holdings in excess of 11,000 hand-written pages.

second version the leader of the guerillas, or perhaps the cap-
tured spy, turns out to be a woman.

Twenty-seven years pass. Rymer visits every conti-
nent on the globe, observes countless savageries, witnesses
cruelty on a scale that, until now, only monsters have chanced
to know. He turns sixty-two and begins to feel anxious and
weary. Every new torture has opened further frontiers. Every master has recounted unimagined feats, exotic lore. And
this has been the great discovery, that instead of an aberra-
tion, torture is a world. It has its high orders and plebeian
class, its schools, geography, gods and epochs. When its history is told, the faithful praise its Renaissance, mourn its dark
times. Rymer now realizes that even the least articulate, most
taciturn excruciator is a virtual cornucopia of disgusting revelations. Torturers want to divulge. Each believes that, alone
among mortals, he or she has experienced what all are mad
to behold. Despite his reverence for these mysteries, Rymer
has begun to worry that they're addictive, that no end to his
research will come, that the future holds no ultimate horror
after which he can stop and tell what he knows.

This fear proves unfounded. For one day on a nameless island in search of a legendary master capable of sus-
taining consciousness during the eating of a vital organ (a
torturer's desideratum that Rymer's journal debunks), Rymer
reaches the conclusion of his work. The celebrated artist is, it
turns out, dead, and if he ever possessed the mythic skill, it
has long since been lost among disciples who, under the influence of Western popular music, no longer discriminate
between torture and gore. Rymer falls in briefly with this
rowdy crew and for the first time in his long career suffers
torture himself. His right ankle is shattered. He loses all vision in one eye and develops a permanent tic. The usable life
of a kidney is reduced. But he survives, and more importantly, he realizes that this experience has consummated his
study. Having crossed the last distance between himself and
all he longed to know, Rymer returns home to write.

This is a terrific plot! The excitement is literally
unbounded. A love interest could develop; I imagine a
Colombian nun, an activist; Rymer botches their one sexual

encounter, and (miscellaneous complications here) she ends up *tortured*! And to offset the misogyny, there could be a revenge scene with feminist vigilantes. A sadistic police chief gets it with a cow prod! Each hardcover sale could contribute a dollar to Amnesty International, and the epigraph might come from Simone Weil or Gandhi. What in the world holds this story back?

There are currently four hypotheses why B. R. Rymer never wrote his study of torture: 1) Rymer's participation in torture may have been more extensive than his records indicate. (He didn't complete his study for fear the truth would come out.) 2) Rymer may never have observed even one act of torture. His thousands of pages of notes make up an elaborate fiction. 3) At some point during the thirty-four years of his study Rymer probably went mad. (The late sixties are often cited.) 4) Rymer may have actually written his study but, because of 1), suppressed its publication. For most of Rymer's critics, 2) has implied 3), and sometimes 1) has implied 3). Of course, 4) depends on 1) and may imply 3).

In my experience, 1) and 4) don't bear discussing. Everything offered as evidence for or against them depends on a prior decision for or against them. However, 2) and 3) are potentially decidable. In most cases, falsifications of records and changes from sane to mad discourse leave traces. In my (less than exhaustive) study of the "1949 Preface," the Wisconsin collection, the Windemeer letters and a few private documents, I haven't found that the internal evidence supports either 2) or 3)[2]. In fact, my interest in Rymer was first aroused by how rapidly, in the absence of evidence, these four hypotheses achieved currency. My hunch was (still is) that their acceptance resulted from my generation's anxiety about its past. I'm convinced that if we lack an explanation for Rymer's silence, it's not because we lack facts. This paradox is, or was to have been, the germ of my novel.

---

[2] This does not deny the abnormality of Rymer's habit, with increasing frequency after the Middle East fieldwork, of referring to himself in the third person.

I imagine it happening this way: upon his return Rymer enters his quantitative data into (the remarkable new invention) a personal computer. The computer generates tables, graphs, diagrams, lists, charts, indexes. Rymer is astonished by the unanticipated regularities that emerge. For example, if the total number, kinds, incidences by year of torture of the sexual organs and the number, kinds, incidences by year of torture of the cerebral region are developed according to the same functions (these are derived from algorithms used to determine stress in expansion bridges), an opposed mirror image of the graphs of their results will form a chiasm. Even more interesting, when the data by continents are organized around certain (exotic) oscillators, the infinite regressions form hyperbolas approaching the north and west. Rymer labors in a perpetual fever. The computer runs night and day. Within four months the calculations have filled his study.

However, as soon as Rymer opens his journal, all work stops. He can make no sense of what he has written. In the midst of a passage about finger-crushing (from the late seventies), the text inexplicably launches a diatribe on musical instruments and Polynesian cosmology. In an earlier section, while describing the boiling of a peasant, the journal gets into a disagreement with Aristotle, and halfway through the only genuine torture of an infant Rymer ever witnessed, he evidently got so irritated with comma conventions that he never completed his notes! The "main point" is rarely extricable from the digressions. Every section spills into every other. (After 1968, all paragraphing stops.) Rymer no longer knows what he was talking about.

He falls into a debilitating malaise. He soon finds that he can work for no more than a couple of hours, sometimes not even an hour. He decides to take a vacation but has already been everywhere in the world, witnessed every excitement. He passes a week sitting in a neighborhood park. At week's end he returns to his journal convinced that he has overlooked something. He reads randomly throughout the three and a half decades. He doesn't find a mistake, but he finds a ghost. The ghost and Rymer have collaborated on the journal. The ghost has observed Rymer from the edge of the circle of pain, but he doesn't know a great deal of what Rymer knows. What Rymer knows is, of course, more enlightening, but the ghost writes better. While following the ghost, Rymer comes across the "1949 Preface." He has completely forgotten about it. He stays up all one night reading and rereading every word. He's overcome with the exhilaration of having discovered a neglected author. At dawn he realizes that the author of the "Preface" is the ghost.

The final scene of my novel occurs in Rymer's neighborhood park. A few years have passed. Rymer has tried every solution to his writer's block, from the most harebrained to the most technical. Gradually, he has resigned himself to the inexplicable, devastating failure of his life. He's a week short of his seventieth birthday, partially disabled, and in perpetual physical discomfort. Sitting on a concrete bench, he feels pressed down by extravagant misfortune. It's nearly midnight. He leans forward, rests his head in his palm, asks why, why. All at once he's struck by the thought that perhaps he's just dead. He looks up at the moon. Death would explain everything! It must've occurred to him on the nameless island where he became the object of his own research. Suddenly, the pain comes crashing back. It's inconceivable. He was sprawled inside a ring of faces, shrill laughter piercing one ear, when he saw, coming toward him, a strange youth demanding freedom. Rymer caught a whiff of burnt meat, opened his mouth to scream. He knew this stranger! Rymer's study of torture was complete.

B. R. Rymer resides in Dubuque, Iowa, a writer of pseudonymous fictions. He is seventy-six years old.[3]

---

[3] (Added to the Revised Edition) Some have misconstrued the foregoing as a defense of all I haven't written. The thought is excruciating to me. Everything I've neglected to say can stand on its own. How could my silence call out for justification? I should've thought all this went without saying.

abandoned writing projects

This is a film. In it, an actor we can't see is arranging small, irregularly shaped objects on a flat surface. The picture's a close-up, focus on what's just appearing, but sometimes the actor shows—his? her?—hand. If we're quick, we catch it breaking the frame. No one can tell for sure what's going on yet, partly because our focus is too narrow. The objects may not be significant; the movements could be a diversion. But we expect this action to lead to something. At the start, watching the film is following it.

The hand stops, the focus enlarges, and the objects lose their strangeness, become an eraser, three bottle caps, a foreign coin, some hair, etc. This change occurs in no time at all, as if underway from the beginning. The image is becoming clearer; the objects are clues. Before we know it, we're wondering: Why a *foreign* coin? Possibly *beer* caps? And just *whose* hair? But by then a voice has taken over, and our attention is being directed.

I say a voice, but not really. That is, the actor doesn't narrate. More like a murmur, run-on, oblivious, hardly more articulate than a groan. He—for with the voice (how has this occurred to us?) we know the hand is male—the actor doesn't

87

address anyone, not even himself. If the film were comic, we'd expect his wife to clear her throat now, say, Dear, your whisssspering again! But no, the murmur, hand, objects— it's all we have to go on.

A pair of scissors enters the frame, blades slightly parted. The hand places them on the surface, then takes the eraser away. Of course, we know scissors are singular, but like binoculars and pants, we call them a pair. They lie on top of the hair now, establishing a connection. The paraphernalia of haircutting? The hair could be a fetish. Or are they for cutting something else?

Suddenly there's a loud thud. The voice rises sharply: Aaaaaay! We wait. Nothing. After several seconds, the hand takes the scissors away.

The surface before us is white. At first, it seems hardly distinguishable from the picture screen, as if all that supported the objects were the wall of the theater itself. Only the shadows of the bottle caps, intimations of depth, suggest a plane distinct from the visual one. But as the picture enlarges, the objects become material, extend into space. At last we can tell that the surface is a desk. Or possibly a drafting table. It stands in front of an open window which is set deep in another wall, this one of white plaster. The window's framed in light wood, hung with gauze curtains. From time to time the curtains stir. A breeze appears to be blowing.

Where? There's a voice. We can hear it. Objects are arranged on a desk. We can see them. A breeze appears to be blowing. We feel nothing. How much farther away this breeze appears than the surface of objects and sounds. Of course, we know projections can be deceiving. Everything before us isn't really happening just as much as everything else, and most of what we can't feel is merely absent, not missing. Still, when the actor's hand vanishes, it has to go somewhere. A frame isn't the end of the world, and most of what's really going on goes on behind the scenes. We sit in our obscurity; the actor labors in another; neither of us starts out with an edge. Can *he* feel the breeze?

A crumpled ball of paper strikes the white surface, or drafting table, bounces up against the wall, rolls to a stop beside the eraser. We tense for another outburst but instead hear—well, a sound.

Of course, there's no end of sounds. The actor's murmur, these chairs creaking, my heartbeats, someone behind me's sniffles, the crunch of candy wrappers under your feet. Even the silence amounts to a roar, discernible in the loud speakers whenever the voice stops. But this sound now is different. Both sharp and muffled, it comes from behind the wall. Two blocks of wood striking, or maybe a firecracker in a can, but happening again and again, sometimes in rapid succession. It reaches us through the window. And even as the actor's hand reappears, huge, ominous, grasping at something yet again, we're moved, or the frame is, translated above the surface, the action, objects, and entering the opening where the breeze blows through.

The film has become the window. The picture's now as big as all outdoors. We can hardly believe our eyes.

A massacre is underway. Wherever we turn, we see forms exploding, automatic weapons retorting, and lifeless figures covering the ground. From a barely visible structure in the distance, smoke rises skyward clouding our view, and moving left to right, a pair of murderers weave their way through the ruins, extinguishing every dying word. We can just make out the last voices, cries exhausting themselves in a final effort to resist annihilation. Everywhere is furor, mayhem, meaningless waste.

Drawn by fear, curiosity, compassion—what draws the eye to scenes of devastation?—the film is bringing us closer. Now the disposition of each body is evident, the tortured expressions, inclinations of head or hand. Nothing remains to be seen, but still we find ourselves almost wholly in the dark. How could all this violence be occurring while the actor in the foreground remains unmoved? Perhaps, in the aftermath of murder, such questions amount to nothing, for plainly any thought of intervening comes too late. Tongues of flame still flicker in the distance, and for a few seconds we hope to discover life among the ruins, but no figure is stirring. All those lying before us now seem inert, their mutilated forms arranged in grotesque attitudes, preposterous positions.

Surveying this holocaust, we can hardly avoid a suspicion of racism, for every character we see is black. Of course, in the heat of conflict, the flesh may have been consumed, or the tragedy, it occurs to us, might be happening elsewhere, in Zaire or Uganda. Not that its location is really material. Genocide is genocide. But we have no idea what state we're in, or why these dead have been sentenced. In the background an arid plateau stretches out of sight, and on the horizon we seem to make out a lavish habitation, although that could be a mirage. But however you look at it, the devastation appears so systematic, so total and unrelenting, that it can't have happened of itself. What plot has the film uncovered? Who's behind it?

No! No! No! the voice suddenly shouts. There's a crash of breaking glass, something strikes against the wall. We'd gotten so absorbed in the devastation before us that we'd lost sight of the actor. Now his proximity is alarming. We wait, the muscles in our legs tensed, hearts pounding. His murmurs don't resume. Was the crash a bullet? And we notice, faintly at first, a new sound, spasmodic, anguished, like panting. Nothing enters our picture. The new sound could be sobbing.

Is the actor's voice black? His ethnicity has never appeared to matter until now, but the identity of those outside the frame is becoming crucial. If the actor's himself a victim, that's one thing, perhaps eluding the authorities or fleeing a sentence awaiting him. Or maybe he's mourning the fallen. Our point of view will be his. But if he's framing this action, then he has a hand in it, and that's something else. Especially if he's white. There's no pretense to be documenting. The first fact is he's nearby and never shows his face. He fiddles with bottle caps, cuts hair, while on the other side of this wall, life as we know it ends.

I've neglected to mention that the film's not in color. This accounts for some of our vagueness. While handling the scissors, the actor momentarily exposed himself, such that, had the picture been other than black and white, we might've decided his race from the start, but now the gray hand has been withdrawn, and there's only a voice to go on.

Can crying have a color? It can certainly have a tone. This crying sounds subdued. Hanging on each gasp, snuffle, wheeze, we listen, determined not to miss a word but quickly losing all sense of what's happening. Like static or white noise, we can't even be sure the voice is human, much less Haitian, Rapper, Anglo, Congolese. Although this ambiguity seems understandable enough—not every issue can be black and white—we know differently. Whatever's screened out, after all, has to be someone's doing, so that, staring at the unmoving figures below, we still feel compelled to make sense. Annihilation can't just go unaccounted for. And if the actor's identified with the murdered, then he's either threatened himself or duplicitous. Our involvement will be the greater. But if he's an outsider, then the film's racism has become transparent, and we'll want to distance ourselves.

The picture is moving again. The camera assumes a superior perspective; the outrage below grows more remote: our horizons expand in every direction. An urban sprawl now encompasses the massacre. We can see that the lifeless forms are lying about what appears to be a deserted project, or possibly a new development that hasn't been completed yet. The lavish habitation formerly on the horizon looks to be a convention center, stylishly made-up figures dashing off in all directions, and the smoking structure has become a hangar or bus terminal. In the foreground stands a badly aging edifice, its façade almost completely worn away, and there are freeways, vacant lots, conflicting signs. Strangely, our higher vantage remains just as focused on the dead figures as before, as though, despite including so much more now, the film still emanated from the violence at its center. How we are to regard this paradox is impossible to say. Apparently, somebody's trying to make a statement, but the picture's tone seems as elusive as the voice's color.

Is our new point of view still the actor's? Up so high we seem to have abandoned his window, but perhaps we're just dreaming. The present perspective could be an unspoken wish, his or ours, to comprehend the devastation on all sides or to take the whole world in. But responsibility for what we see is becoming difficult to assign. For all we know, we could be God looking down on our, such as it is, creation, or perhaps this lofty vision is a birdbrain's. Of course, technology may have lifted us above ourselves again—Could that window at the edge of the frame be the opening we just passed through? And could the blank face looking this way be him? After all, the wish for transcendence is only human. But however you look at it, all we see is all we see, nobody else appearing to have a hand in our picture, and all we hear is the wind, fragile soprano rising and falling or the occasional explosion when a gust hits the microphone.

In the city, life goes on. An elevated train glides over the lifeless project, and traffic lines the freeway just as if genocide were an everyday affair. The occasional passerby can be seen to stick a head out—white? black? Up so high, which of us can tell? But there's no indication of alarm. Ambulances don't come screaming to the rescue. The only police car is mired in gridlock. It's as if down below everybody's watching a movie, or as if the dying forms had become invisible. We strain our eyes to detect the slightest movement, maybe a scavenger sifting the wreckage or a fugitive trying to escape, but nothing moves except our eyes. The gunshots have stopped, or anyway their reports no longer reach us. Among the lifeless figures, not a soul stirring.

One thing's impossible to miss, however: the disaster isn't natural. Perhaps it's the cosmopolitan environs, the modernity and nearby motion, or maybe it's that the tragedy appears so localized, but the unmoving characters look increasingly artificial. Whereas at first their dispositions seemed accidental, each falling as its gravity determined, now every demise seems arranged. The contorted heads and torsos parody a human being's collapse, and the attitudes in which the extremities are displayed appear ludicrously contrived. Even their expressions, which at our present distance we no longer try to make out, come back to us as staged. I have a confession to make. Gazing at these figures, I get the uncanny feeling that, at any instant, they could return to life. I find it literally incredible that lifeless forms are all I can see. If I'm to be frank, my hallucination will sound madder still. It's that the instant before I turn my eyes upon the figures, they are full of feeling, and that the instant I turn aside, they recover all their senses again, but that my eternal curse, or theirs or maybe just the film's, is that I have only to dwell upon them for all that holds my attention to be spirited away. Of course, this could be no more than my consciousness that, after all, I'm looking at a film, not out a window. Or out the latter only in the former, or the former merely figured as the latter, I mean figured formally, or as the latter formerly figured, or former, but all the same, the violence on the screen is being projected. Turn the lens aside and the dead will rise, make wisecracks and trouble, flirt, fornicate, renegotiate their contracts, demand artistic representation. If so much is obvious, why does it feel disappointing?

Suddenly in the theater—How's this possible?—a chair scrapes across the floor and someone nearer than the breeze blows his nose right in our ear. Footsteps are approaching from the loud speaker. Everybody tenses. What's happening? And then there's a tympanum-shattering crash. Our picture goes crazy. The city inverts, buildings and bodies start to whirl, the whole earth's spinning—Are we staring into a clothes dryer?—and the screen turns black. Shit shit shit shit shit shit shit shit! we hear a voice, sounds like the same again, muttering. For a few seconds there's this repetitive theater-shaking thud, like someone beating his head against a wall. Then nothing. We half expect the credits to roll. We can't just picture ourselves sitting in the dark like this, but how can we tell if what started is over? Even this now could be more of it.

Maybe what feels so disappointing is that the actor is white. Just how we can tell would be hard to tell, but from his obscenities, all those in the know, both white and black, know. That the one in hiding is not among the victims is what nobody sitting in front of this blank screen can now fail to see. This alters everyone's perspective. Evidently, the individual who framed our picture expects us to find genocide entertaining. Doesn't he know that on our side of the lens the world's in color? Every second we remain in the dark our presence is compromising, but leaving at this point means never knowing what the killing makes all but intolerable not to know.

No roar of the sound track. The surrounding blackness isn't projected. People have started to talk. Seats creaking, somebody hissing, feet in the aisle. A candy wrapper whizzes past. Christ, what are we waiting for?

When the picture finally returns, it's moving again. Rising above the city and its dead, we watch as our world's edge slips away, revealing a limitless horizon. For an instant the screen feels unsupported, as though the theater were no longer backing it, leaving us giddy—are we free at last or falling as never before?—but as the unbroken vista expands, we gaze out at just what is hard to say. Everything appears illuminated, but nothing's particularly enlightening any more. As far as the eye can see is neither light nor dark nor white nor black nor admixture nor absence but only what, unpictured, appears to go without saying and, pictured, hardly matters at all. Does this mean the film has covered everything? Looking at nothing in particular we seem to detect a universal brilliance, a slick sheen on every surface that makes the picture's object hard to grasp. We want to get a grip on this film, peel it away, but not to discover what's behind it—So far into the reel, we aren't still hoping to uncover a plot—nor to expose the actor's hand—Could anything be emptier? The screen appears so lucid and unobjectionable now, so precisely as we'd like, or anyway, so precisely not as we'd not like, that what's still the matter is hard to put your finger on. The surface of our planet down below appears so smooth, so glossy and seamless that, if its balance were ever disturbed, we'd have nothing to cling to. Or only politics, since the film's racism, if racism's what it projects, can hardly prove as groundless as the film. But the killer is, nothing blocks our view now but our view. If, in spite of all, we find ourselves still wanting, how can we tell if what we want is more?

Before us is the screen.

Seconds pass. Unbroken vistas, limitless expanse, unimaginable brilliance.

We wait. Nothing appears to hold our attention. Air enters my lungs. My blood stirs. Air escapes my lips. What's happened to the breeze?

Then without our knowing, we're off. Horizons start to converge, the light's vanishing point vanishes, the earth edges closer, clouds, smoke, former perspective returns, overlooking cityscape and genocide, focus narrowing on ruins, black figures, smoldering remains, until, startling us with the window's familiar confinement, our frame and wall, we alight at last on the white surface from which we departed. There's a tangle of dark string or yarn beside the bottle caps now, one end passing out of the frame at the right. Also a green dispenser of cellophane tape. The coin is missing. A fourth cap has been added. For no apparent reason, I find my body relaxing.

The sound of a voice.

Look, how much longer do you expect them to wait?

It's a woman's. Maybe not Anglo, but maybe nothing else. Her words are the first—the first since no and shit—to reach us.

Three seconds, a long sigh. Is there something I'm supposed to say?

It's just a picture, for God's sake, not the end of—

They're dead. Don't you get it? All of them. Dead.

We hear her pace. How do you stand it in here? It's so stuffy!

Something's happened. If you'll go back to the beginning—

The beginning? Mother of God.

The window sash sliding. Where'd this broken glass come from? she asks.

Open, closed, you never feel any breeze, he says.

Altered tone. No matter what you think, people aren't oblivious. Really. They care. But these problems are just *yours,* and you can't expect—

But they're *my* problems....

Exactly. And you can't expect—

But they're *my* problems....

Exactly. And you can't expect—

Stoppit stoppit. Between me and...okay, I know you know, but there's this white rectangle. From where I sit, it's in front of everybody else too, as if, like, we'd all have to overlook what's staring us in the face just to get through to each other, but I feel, and I can't account for this, I know it's crazy, I feel—wouldn't it be crazier to never say so?—I feel completely abandoned, or nearly, or anyway that's what I call how it feels whenever I face the rectangle, maybe it's how everybody feels, but who knows why, I simply can't get around it. I mean it's a goddamn white rectangle! Well, since the only thing we see eye-to-eye on is that no white rectangle, however you figure it, will ever hold anyone's interest long, it does nobody any good to say, hey look, it's a white rectangle. But since the white rectangle's all I can ever see, well, it's not like I can just say, how 'bout them scissors!

There's so much more to life than string and bottle caps.

Do you really think I need someone to tell me that?

Peremptory snort. All right then, I'm giving you ten lines. Let's see what can you do?

Do?

Do.

Do?

Do!

"Do"?

"DO"!

"DO"?

Don't!

Don't?

Aaaaaaaaaaargh! The door slams, footsteps echo down a hall.

Our focus narrows, the hand appears again, huge now, filling the picture. It fiddles with the yarn, picks up the scissors, hesitates over the yarn, puts down the scissors. Three more seconds. Then the sound of a chair scraping, door opens, closes, footsteps—heavier this time—fading in the hall.

We find ourselves abandoned. The objects before us mere objects. The breeze, if there's any breeze, unfelt. No telling what's to follow. Only the frame still moves, or perhaps the tape, yarn, caps do, no more than a shiver at first, then everything goes wobbly, focus slowly traversing the seam of desk and wall, horizontal to vertical, or theoretically, since hovering who knows how far away now, our third dimension has collapsed, picture going flat, so that, gradually inverting us, depending on where we are, that is, our picture simply leaves everything up in the air. The wall becomes the wall. Roar of the sound track stops. On all sides black or white. Or nothing.

This is not a film.

free enterprise

The head of Coca-Cola makes more than Nicaragua. The most profitable business in America is hospitals. While losing more than Michigan, General Motors paid its CEO more than the police. A neurosurgeon's coffee break would cost you your life. Instead of building a nuclear sub, America could build almost anything. Every citizen threatens to be more trouble than she's worth. If the federal budget were used to buy Microsoft, it wouldn't. Children make poor investments. Madonna has just purchased Prague.

Numbers beat Jesus. I wake up reckoning, figure all night more or less, more or less. Talk of values may be cheap, but I'm pretty sure price tags can be counted on. As I've told Deirdre, all anyone wants is his fair share, which in my case I've calculated to five decimals, but she just lies on her pillow dreaming. She wants an ocelot, she says, a coyote or a kestrel. Nature's invaluable, I know, to be preserved at all costs, but predators, even *small* predators, well, aren't they another story? What about the parrot, I plead, what about the kitties and terrier? But in the darkness I hear her crooning, love, love, love. Is wildlife what we've bought into? Is Deirdre's consumption the bottom line? Five of nine marriages end in bloody divorce, a terrifying carnage. The waste, I'm told, is unavoidable, but when the price of survival gets too high, I tell myself stories to go back to sleep.

The justice system goes bankrupt. The Attorney General huddles with Congress, people at her bus stop, the housekeeper, then calls a press conference.

"The rich are above the law!" she announces.

The reporters screw up their faces. "This is news?"

The AG consults an aide, there's some muttering, then her cab driver leans toward the microphone. "It's a policy," he explains, "not a confession."

Statistics have come to the rescue. Countless tax dollars each year are wasted prosecuting rich criminals, and to what end? Faced with nationwide collapse and depression, our leaders acknowledge the obvious. If there's no holding the rich accountable, why not just say so?

As the AG explains, any citizen indicted of a crime is now allowed to stand trial for his crime or his fortune. Prosecutors have similar options. If convicted of wealth, the citizen becomes Officially Above the Law, or OFFAL, and can never be prosecuted again. The courts wash their hands of him.

This will save millions! The rich will stop trying to justify themselves, and no prosecutor will feel forced by public outrage to throw tax dollars away. The courts can return to the legitimate business of incarcerating the defenseless, and because wealth is no longer on trial, attorneys' fees will plummet. Everybody wins! The police escort the OFFAL as far as the courthouse foyer. After that he's free.

The first test of the new policy occurs in North Carolina where several tobacco executives convicted of wealth have retreated onto fortified estates patrolled by private armies. Corporate in-fighting breaks out, and during a hostile takeover the workers are caught in the crossfire and wiped out. The non-unionized police offer token resistance to the private military contractors but rapidly come to terms. In the financial chaos twelve innocent retirees are destroyed. Because all those responsible are above the law, no crime is committed, but the local citizenry is understandably upset.

Also, the continuing presence of such extra-legal force threatens a serious destabilization of the natural survival struggle that undergirds the region's economy. A grass roots buy-out effort fizzles when the department of commerce doesn't recognize OFFAL, and an abortive night-raid in hot-air balloons leaves the families of five employees without health insurance. Once again wealth appears to have won the day.

But the American genius for exploiting misfortune soon comes to the rescue. From its inception the new jurisprudence has foundered on the problem of inheritance above the law. Technically speaking, fortunes outside the court's jurisdiction can't be willed, and as a practical matter the government has frequently had to take over the effects of dead OFFAL to prevent mayhem. This raises the specter of foreign intervention and threatens to force rich criminals back into court. But a little known attorney in a North Carolina public defender's office sees in this legal incoherence a solution to the dangers of corporate warfare. She proposes airdropping into a tobacco executive's fortress five thousand leaflets articulating a new policy on extra-legal estates: to wit, in the event of wealth's demise, the OFFAL remains will be appropriated by the local authorities and divided equitably among the OFFAL's domestic employees. Within forty-eight hours one hundred and ninety-two private paramilitary units appear at the county sheriff's office bearing the bullet-riddled bodies of the tobacco executi

Was that pain?

Deirdre has sat up in bed.

I try to stop lying to myself. Pain?

Listen.

Silence, tree frogs, crickets, flying squirrels, tom cat, pack of beagles, barred owl half a mile away.

I thought I heard an animal, she says. Suffering, I mean.

Don't nightmares count?

Not if you're the animal.

I gaze up from my pillow. Y'know, if humans had only eight fingers, they'd probably count on base eight instead of ten. Not like they'd actually say eight instead of ten,

but the number after seven would be, y'know, ten. So really
they'd—

We'd.

—we'd still be counting on base ten, only ten would
mean eight. Now if there was this tribe with twelve fingers
and they had a number, say, ogle, after nine and another, say,
whippet, before ten, they'd laugh at the rest of us for calling
ogle ten, but still we'd all be counting on base—

Do they hurt you?

Silence, pond frogs, cicadas, screech owl, doves coo-
ing, more crickets, bats, foxes yipping somewhere, cat fight.

Your fingers I mean. Is that why you rub them?

They itch. A little. Must be a tic or—

Here, let me get some lotion.

But the point is, I call after her, nobody knows what
they're worth, or anything is, since, if there were more fingers, or less, ten could be eight or twelve or thirty or—

She's back. Sometimes I start thinking about how
many deer and foxes and possums and rabbits get fleas or
heartworms or scabies or worse with nobody there to rub—

So like Bill Gates, maybe he really doesn't have more
money than Ethiopia, he's just got fewer fingers, so he counts
to ten faster, while Ethiopia—

Give me your hands.

I can't sleep like that.

Sleep? You were asleep?

I mean dream. With you holding my hands, I-I can't
dream.

I can. I want a baby ferret.

blic defender's stratagem undergoes subsequent
modification—especially to accommodate shifts from private
armies to terrorist cadres underwritten by innovative life
insurance—the basic principal, that of competing for the productive labor of citizens who thrive on OFFAL, triumphs
again and again. In the majority of cases, rich criminals, once
declared above the law, seek anonymity and happily relin-
quish their interest in the economic well-being of others.

This remarkable success story results directly from the
new policy's upbeat, pro-American emphasis. As Attorney

General Alfreda Gilmore explains, "For public management professionals like myself, the rich have long been a problem. Laws don't scare them, there's nothing they can conceivably want. They wouldn't be caught dead in your pathetic schools. In general, they're impervious to the rewards and threats we use to control the rest of you." She gives the reporters a cheekbone shot, flashes explode. "In our professional opinion this deviation from behavior the majority of Americans find beneficial constitutes a syndrome: Lengthy and Abundant Personal Security Surplus, or LAPS. What has long been needed to rehabilitate the rich is exposure to what we call the Great American Project of Personal Survival, or GAPS. Once above the law, the LAPS of the wealthy can be reinvigorated by the GAPS. Each day becomes a genuine adventure. Personal culture fades, and the rich rediscover the thrill of fighting for their lives!"

However, the AG's plan owes its immediate popularity less to this exciting frontier spirit than to a sixty-two-year-old laid-off factory worker, Bela Wachowski who, leaving for the firearms store one afternoon, receives a phone call from Oprah. She's interviewing the nation's distraught. He can tell his story to the world! It's a miracle!

As Wachowski explains to a daytime tv audience: "The problem with this country, see, is gov'ment. I mean, I don't blame the bosses. They got a problem with some employee—say the guy's a bum—can't fire him. Regulations. And then there's feds, snoops."

"This is very, very impressive, don't you agree, folks?" Oprah turns to the studio audience. Thunderous applause. "A man like Mr. Wachowski, suffering from… well, pessimists might call it our system's failure, but you, sir, still maintain your faith, your hope—"

"America, see, wasn't it built with folks' two hands? Okay, but now, us who made it, nobody can defend his legimit interests. Man's gotta protect his family, his property. A business losin' money, laws shouldn't get in the way. A guy losin' his job, laws shouldn't get in the way. Everybody lookin' out for his own self. Ain't that a free country?"

Of course, many economists disapprove of Wachowski's private initiative. They point out that, having already lost his livelihood, Mr. Wachowski can profit little from terminating those responsible—surely death threats will not make him more attractive to future employers!—and so his reasoning, by confounding a desire for retribution with the profit motive, actually makes little economic sense. In fact, questions about the theoretical incompatibility of justice systems and economic systems seem, at the outset, the only source of articulate criticism of the OFFAL policy. As one disgruntled liberal economist puts it, "Hell, even the fucking president is rich!" To which it is rejoined that said chief executive has repeatedly shown himself above the law.

However, it is not long before a more serious challenge arises within the courts themsel

I heard it again! Deirdre is on her feet this time, wrestling into her robe. I-I'm going out there.

I struggle to accommodate this new horror: Dee, it's only the food chain for Christ's sake!

Humans can live on sour barley and pro football. Why can't foxes learn to eat bean curd?

Look, do you have any idea how many people are being tortured right now in Sarajevo? Do you know the number of lives our breakfast cereal could save?

No, thank Goddess, and neither does anyone else. She clicks on the closet light. Where's that dog snare?

It could be a cougar. It could turn on you.

Everything's gotta eat. She pulls a long pole with a noose at one end from the closet. Seems like I remember last time this thing didn't work.

Talk to me, I say. Isn't the real problem with the world today war, disease, famine? I mean, three centuries ago, they could be counted on, right, but now humans're like bunnies without bobcats. There's an equation, you've seen it, how fast deer will gnaw the planet clean if we don't blow their heads off.

She pauses at the door. Don't talk to me like I'm crazy, R—. You know I'm not what's crazy. *It* is.

Silence, bull frog, whip-poor-will, cicadas, bats, crickets, doves, screech owl, luna moth flapping at the porch light.
member of the studio audience
Mark Register
Lotta Cash
Lisa Carr
unemployed computer technician from
Anita Faber
Matt Downs
Nope, nope, nope.
"intiative won't even amount to"
Linda Hand
doesn't count
Willa Kerr
"this just be wasting money on rich trials?"

Kerr's remark goes unremarked at the time, but six months into the policy's implementation, it's quoted again and again. For no sooner does the AG's cab driver complete his OFFAL explanation for the press, than an unprecedented outpouring of corporate largesse to law colleges begins. Prestigious new RICH chairs are endowed, foundations arise for the jurisprudence of wealth, and fellowships become available for pioneering research into indefensible money. After scarcely four months of OFFAL trials, the depressing spectacle of limousines dropping off putative bag ladies at courthouses becomes commonplace, and prosecutors begin to speculate that old-fashioned criminal prosecution may be easier. The former wasteful, unjust, and over-regulated legal system seems to be reproducing itself.

But once again, Yankee ingenuity—that American blend of bold initiative, independent viewpoint, and ceaseless calculation—saves the day. As many have observed, Attorney General Gilmore is herself not above a suspicion of wealth, but even her harshest critics agree that she certainly knows her lawyers. In a single daring stroke she restores what has now begun to be called Wachowski's Initiative to its original intent by authoring legislation that transforms OFFAL trials into experiments in primitive democracy. After centuries hiding behind subsidiaries and articles of incorporation, the rich will finally represent themselves.

Although controversial, her proposal finds surprising support among legal experts. Where the sole question is wealth, they reason, guilt and innocence are not at issue. Having been accused of no crime, the rich are exempt from the constitutional guarantee of counsel. The sole purpose of OFFAL trials is to determine community perception. As Attorney General Gilmore explains, "It's not that ordinary citizens always know who's rich. It's that Americans mistaken for powerful become so. Why else would there be advertising?" Although she concedes that being judged wealthy might not be identical with possessing a fortune, it almost certainly means OFFAL is above the law. "There've always been two courts in this country," she explains. "We're just legalizing public opinion."

The practical arrangements take awhile to sort themselves out. The earliest OFFAL trials still resemble trials. Witnesses, evidence and cross-examinations all follow the familiar television format. However, with time, the new form begins to assert itself. Inspirational anecdotes and *ad hominem* attacks replace legalese. Courtroom maneuvers not familiar from "L.A. Law" and "Matlock" are abandoned. Wealthy defendants find themselves undone, not by wily litigators, but by folk etymology and backporch demagogues, and in a misguided upsurge of interest in popular persuasion, American English departments become for a few confused weeks the astonished recipients of panicked philanthropy. However, it becomes rapidly apparent that, be they ever so mercenary, modern poets are a liability in any struggle. No one knows why, but no sooner is anything theirs to defend, than

Deirdre's holding a baby chipmunk.

Horned owl? I ask. King snake?

Sourpuss, she says.

Our neighbor's cat. She holds the creature under the night light, and for several seconds we don't speak, listening to it breathe. Then we swing into motion. I find a box, fill it with towels, hook up the heat lamp. Deirdre warms some goat milk, digs the eyedropper out, makes a hospital of the kitchen. We put the dog in the yard, shut the kittens in the bedroom. The chipmunk breathes on. We decide he's unharmed but seriously terrified. We have no idea what to do, of course, so we begin to watch. Exactly what we're watching for, why watching for it matters, or how we'll know if it arrives, are all questions we don't entertain. We sit there. The periodic lurch of the tickless clock-hand drowns out every other noise, either imaginary or the alternative to imaginary. Time passes, I reckon.

Finally, as natural as disaster, Deirdre begins dreaming. She wants a zoo, she tells me for the nth time, but not just any zoo, a conservation ecologist's hallucination of the classless state. Every being in its own habitation, nobody eats anybody, macrobiotic cornucopia, all life thriving together apart. You can't tame wild creatures, I of course for the nth time tell her, and, what *can* you tame then, she for the nth time retorts. We exchange those old looks that say, you're not really going to start this over again, are you? And I relent and she continues. In Deirdre's zoo, leopards will dote on tofu, and crocodiles'll spend the afternoon bobbing for yogurt balls. Even the mosquitoes will be happy somehow. Blood drives maybe. It's a grain-eater's utopia, hegemony of the local healthfood store, with just enough dairy to keep the proteins whole. Imagine, she tells me, if carnivores could do it, there might be hope for humans. Which evidently she considers a good thing. I do my best not to humor her but find sanity unrewarding. Outside, the night has gone silent. Around two a.m. our eyes won't keep open so we decide to tuck the chipmunk in and go back to sleep. Sleep. For a few precious hours I know nothing. When a little before five I get up to pee, it's dead.

> my life savings
> teller's window
> declining rate of interest
> wouldn't bank on it
> credit my account
> at all costs
> Minny Nichols

Wilma Fortune
Cassius Littleworth
Ira Ward
free market economist
"the immense natural resource of an armed citizenry"
surprising support for Wachowski's initiative across
the political spectrum. Despite the reform's tendency to increase the vulnerability of capital, many at the University of
Chicago have been enthusiastic. "For the first time the economic potential of our homicide rate has been recognized,"
says Nobel Laureate Ira Ward Moore. "Quite spontaneous
acts of acquisition and liquidation are being harnessed to
productive ends. Why, it's a new frontier!" Along with others who have wished to encourage innovation and give wider
play to the market's normal fluctuation, Dr. Moore has ap-
plauded Wachowski's pioneering spirit. Unlike the present
system in which risk decreases as it is rewarded, Dr. Moore
explains, the Wachowski system rewards and increases risk
simultaneously. "What is different, what is genuinely fresh
and, I must say, astonishing is that freedom and danger no
longer diverge. Citizens are free to acquire to their heart's
content, but few will remain fierce for deregulation."

Although debate continues over how much real freedom those above the law enjoy, it's estimated that during
the first three years of this nationwide conservation effort,
the country's OFFAL has been reduced by forty-nine percent. Of the rubbish about whose removal reliable information exists, between eighty and eighty-four percent have been
eliminated through the voluntary efforts of private citizens.
At present twenty-nine cases of waste have been disposed
of between the courthouse foyer and their cars

No no no no no.
liberal commentator Pollyanna Severance
Felicity Woodstock
and sixties activist
Sonny Mourning
"Wow! I mean, really, are we talkin' revolutionary or
what, huh? I mean, it's just a, y'know, kinda coup d'état
thing. Except it's all legal, almost, or sort of. Anyway, it's

not *il*legal. Power to the people and all that! I mean, really, wow!"

God.

I suppose even the most determined dream won't stay aloft indefinitely. Having soothed my heart with orgies of revenge, mine seems to be plummeting toward catastrophe as predictably as an anvil. Be realistic, I hear a voice cry, and then in the distance: Abandon hope, all ye who enter here! The poor get poorer, the rainforests vanish, nuclear holocaust proves inevitable. And five of nine times Deirdre leaves me for good. I know this voice can't be my voice, but I also know it can't be other.

The decisive challenge to Wachowski's Initiative arises from the source of its power, the American people. In New Hampshire a journalist stirs up controversy when he refuses to disclose the source of information in a murder investigation. The murderer gets off and, six hours later, rapes and kills the eighteen year old truckstop waitress who accused him. The journalist is charged with contempt. Old political animosities surface; he makes an insensitive remark; a radio evangelist preaches a sermon against him, and surprise surprise, the prosecution tries him as OFFAL. It's a joke, of course. The reporter's salary's peanuts. But then there's a family business and some life insurance and this one year he didn't pay taxes and...well, the boyfriend of the waitress is waiting on the courthouse steps. Ker-pow-eee.

The shooting occurs live on national TV. A chill runs through the nation. An emergency wealth conference is held. Oprah attends. The AG brings her cab driver. In his stirring keynote address, Bela Wachowski demands: "How come, just 'cause this guy wears a tie, y'know, he takes food out my gran'baby's mouth, takes my hospitalization, but then soon's I try to defend my int'ress, this cop he comes up an' says where ya goin' with that pistol?" But the country's just not hip anymore. Mysterious words like "regressive" and "savagery" begin to pop up in perfectly sensible conversations, and former presidential advisor and popular game-show host, I. M. "Rob" Goodrich, in his last public appearance, goes so far as to brand Wachowski's initiative "bad for the ratings." The next day Goodrich and four other prominent nay-sayers receive parking tickets. The local DA tries them as OFFAL. None survives the conference.

Pretty soon any suspension of calculation looks OF-FAL. Paranoia sets in. Neighbors begin to oversee each other, laptops open on their knees. The worth of every second is determined to the mill, and time spent on unrewarding interests becomes evidence of hidden resources. Reading subtitles in a French movie, although no crime, is an indulgence few can see the value of, and dwelling on puns or double entendres seems a conspicuous consumption characteristic of only the richest lives. Unappreciated behavior begins to add up. Priceless moments yield no return. Although most still feel that what individuals do in their free time is their business, all agree that business, when profitable, should be taxed, and if a private concern persists with no profit to show, then a public accounting is to be feared. In the wee hours of the night, police cars are seen cruising lightless neighborhoods, soft knocks can be heard at the door. There's an unpaid speeding ticket from Billings, Montana, and this guy who says he sold you marijuana three decades ago, and a warrant for the arrest of someone with your name fitting your description who injured a woman remarkably like a woman you loved but in a state you've never entered in a time before you wer

You can't just keep cramming me into your nightmares like this! Deirdre's awake.

I shrug. Frames invade pictures. Whatever's happening that's still happening discredits whatever's happening that's—

The chipmunk's dead, isn't it?

I nod, or maybe I just stare back.

She doesn't flinch. When you think about, it's a relief. I mean, death's like a dream. It happens without you.

I wouldn't count on that.

Sometimes I can't wait.

What you and I spend on toilet paper would clothe a Thai village. Without poverty we'd never eat fresh grapes.

Some nightmares you'd have to be asleep not to reckon with, but dying—well, once you start counting there's just no end of it.

Deirdre watches me watch her watch me. Aren't there incalculable terrors you'd give anything to preserve?

At what cost?

Then in a face that regularly looks pretty crazy, I see something happening that I think, shit, that looks pretty crazy.

Meow, she says.

I laugh, sort of. Not that I never lie to myself about dying—

Deirdre's hackles rise. She crawls closer.

—or try, but it's never dying, not really, or not me, or worse, it's never *you* dying, which is what I really never lie to myself about, what I lie about everything else instead of lying to myself about, I mean, lying about everything else is mostly what—

Grrrrrrrrrrr. I feel what I think must be nibbling on my neck.

—but then on the news or in the paper there'll be this number, thirty-nine perish in flames, two hundred twenty-three bodies found in the wreckage, three thousand believed lost, six million, six million, six million—a genuinely unimaginable number that, if only I could count to a hundred in under a minute and keep on counting to every successive hundred in under a minute and maintain this breakneck rate of counting to a hundred every minute without pause eight hours every day, would take me just over four months to count to—six million tortured and murdered, and every one one just like you and I are one, or both ones, or each a one, or maybe not like, but then isn't dying all one, so that when I try to lie to myself six million times more terrifyingly about dying than I'm already too terrified to lie to myself about even once—

Deirdre's face is beside my face, her breath in my ear. You could be inside me right now, she whispers. Your flesh could be my flesh, blood my body, your taste on my tongue. Who knows how many deaths are alive under my skin?

The world doesn't have to be like this! I shout.

And then she bites me.

YEOWWWWWWWWWW!

I exist.

If history's what hurts, maybe it's what matters, too. Lying doesn't bring me relief. Who can tell why? But in the morning if, against all odds, Deirdre's still lying beside me, well, how come everything's not possible?

Oooee! Oooee! Oooee! I'm bouncing around on the bed, trying to stanch the blood streaming from my neck.

Okay, we're going to finish this together, she says, and then my accounting resumes in an unknown voice.

A convoy of armored cars transporting America's gold bullion for its annual cleaning makes a wrong turn in Albuquerque and disappears into a space warp. The sky's a gorgeous blue. Children breathe air no one has ever breathed before. Across the planet price tags are suddenly meaningless. In the ladies room at the Tokyo exchange, dollar bills replace the toilet tissue. The head of EXXON undergoes an identity crisis. In Times Square parties break out: democracy is coming to America!

Unfortunately, nobody can tell what anything's worth. Little red sports cars briefly cost more than cantaloupes, but for no apparent reason. On the black market, the price of clean water abruptly skyrockets. Crisp lettuce looks sexier than tight buns, and on one amazing Thursday morning in October the whole nation decides there's no reason to get out of bed.

It's chaos, of course, but for those already living this way, it's fun. The national savior, Mr. Wachowski, runs for president on a "let's just shoot everybody" ticket, but then two months pass without oil imports, so who gives a shit? People can't get to their jobs. Factories shut down. In Detroit the homeless people protest: "We were here first!" Some riots break out over the best sidewalk grates and cardboard boxes. There are food fights in California and New Mexico, rumors of massacres of telecommunications executives. A Nobel laureate gets caught looting a convenience store. Heart surgeons panhandle in the subways, but everybody's polite to them. When a convoy of fresh vegetables runs out of gas in Nebraska, even the National Guard quits. Then things get bad.

The family farms are all gone, and the company farms are too big to run without gasoline. There's a drought. About a hundred-ninety thousand famished advertising professionals line up to jump off skyscrapers in Manhattan. As people begin to starve, the chair of Mitsubishi and a San Diego narcotics dealer named Pasquale find they have a lot in common. Hungry and desperate, they and thousands like them start acting like a family. The last resources are precious. So little must go so far.

Who can take charge in this crisis? all families wonder. Who knows how to run everybody's business for them, give orders, tend a garden, survive on a budget, cook dinner, and who, when we felt defeated, hurt, scared, and lonely, never failed to raise our sagging spirits again?

Grandmothers come to the rescue. They snatch the guns from the foreheads of suicidal millionaires and show them how to hoe a tomato patch. They make their daughters take off those silly business suits and dry the dishes. Wherever young men have gone soft and whiny, they pet them and say how strong and brave they are, then remind them that the gate needs mending. There's a lot of grumbling, needless to say, but at eleven o'clock in the corridor as the indignant women, all wives now, and worthless men, all somebody's husband, lumber toward their rooms, granny still has the gall to make a remark about conjugal obligations. For about four minutes the whole nation bounces in bed like a dinghy. None of us knows why we obey her.

It's a reactionary outrage! Women in the kitchen, men in the field! What could be more arbitrary, not to mention plain old-fashioned oppressive? Granny's a goddamn meddling tyrant, but Christ, she has put *food* on our table! And in the last nanosecond before sleep, when the demands of bellies and love and children have been silenced and each one's own happiness looks like the most preposterous illusion, in that firing of a synapse just before passing from the world, you recall your former dream in which this narrow bed wasn't home. There are nights when that old dream seems a thousand times more real than anything you can touch. But then you wake up, and it's morning again, and there's work, food, water, birth, love, dying—and not a second to lose. Well, we're sure gonna do things differently, we all mutter, when we're back on our own again, but for now—hey, could you hand me that ladle?

So at the banquet of the whole nation, as all our relations join to break bread, Granny stomps out of the kitchen and calls for everybody to pay attention. "Mr. Wachowski, give thanks," she orders, and amid coughs, suppressed giggles, and universal eye-rolling, Wachowski stands. Exactly what or why or who he's supposed to thank, nobody's really sure, but he starts talking just the same. "...I keep lookin' at de food. And I think, well, who woulda believed? I gotta confess. I used to be rich. I had a house, didn't own it just me, but there's this bank, y'know, and I had a boy, Jody, lived seventeen years. My boy. Seventeen years. And me and my wife weren't in love exactly but...." He coughs, blushes. "Well, thanks for the bread. Let's eat."

There's a rattle of cutlery, laughter, squeaking of chairs from Amherst to Seattle, then nothing. America waits. And as we all poise before the accident of survival, we know our story doesn't have to end this way.

samuel beckett's
Middlemarch

To attribute the *Imitatio Christi* to Louis Ferdinand Céline or to James Joyce, is this not a sufficient renovation of its tenuous spiritual indications?

—Borges

When rumors of an unpublished, twelve-hundred page Beckett MS first started to circulate, Beckett's admirers were unsure how to react. At first, a hoax was suspected, and then, after Beckett's literary executors made their initial disclosures, accusations of fraud and tampering filled *TLS*. However, no depth of suspicion could have prepared readers for the shock attendant upon the work's publication. Public consternation was aptly expressed in Sir Arthur Dilbeck's remark, "If *this* is Beckett, nobody knew the other one."

In general, the subsequent eight years have normalized this confusion without relieving it. After the waves of hysteria and outrage subsided, critical response to what is clearly Beckett's most bewildering, and arguably his most ambitious, novel retreated into three familiar positions:

1) The work is a failure, the result of Beckett's poor health and intermittent senility.

This judgment was first put forth by Jean Louis Duboer and the circle of Paris bohemians intimately associated with the author during his declining years. In Duboer's scabrous *Le Monde* editorial, Beckett's posthumous work was the "nostalgique et vulgaire" self-indulgence of a badly deteriorated genius in continuous physical agony. In his lucid moments, Beckett recognized its inferiority. It was never intended for publication. Beckett's executors had overstepped. Despite leaving the novel's obvious artistry unaccounted for, Duboer's explanation seemed initially convincing, in part due to the quantity of anecdotal evidence he (and later Martin Crock) produced in its support.

Although Duboer's intent was to preserve Beckett's reputation, his testimony actually played into the hands of those forces of reaction who, since the early seventies, had sought to discount the author's writing. By suggesting that *any* of Beckett's texts could result from physical, mental, or moral deterioration, the Duboer circle unwittingly drove the first nail into their friend's coffin. Almost at once the symptomologies of *Endgame* and *Murphy* began to appear. If degeneracy had produced prose as lucid as Beckett's epic of a latter day St. Theresa, then what of the unintelligibilities in *How It Is*? Soon Beckett's decriers were knocking at the gates of *Godot* itself, ready to consign even this most masterful Beckettian creation to the confines of Bedlam.

2) Beckett's last novel is a parody, written to affront his idolatrous followers.

It was in response to this genuinely disturbing wave of bourgeois *ressentiment* that Beckett's most indefatigable, if not his most inspired interpreters, Professors Jujube Paul and Erich Politbeer, bethought themselves of a new course. Paul and Politbeer's *Mal One Dies: Beckett's Last Laugh*, the first book-length study of the posthumous novel, and nine months later, D. J. Fischkart's *Mortifying Remains*, both presented what most have taken to be irrefutable evidence that Beckett's late turn cannot be attributed to senility. Beckett had actually conceived the novel as early as 1969 and may have completed a draft during the same period that he was at work on *Pas*. Its focus on "reform" was actually a none-too-veiled mockery of the utopian schemes introduced after the 1968 Paris uprisings, and its saintly protagonist carica-tured the "Christian existentialism" of the day, in particular, that of one egregiously earnest American scholar, Dorothy Rivers (Cf. Dorothea Brooke), whose now forgotten mono-graph, "Onward Christian Soldiers: The Forward March of Beckett's Middle Years," appeared in October of 1969, a month before Beckett's first sketch of the novel.

Paul and Politbeer's meticulous dating of Beckett's drafts effectively undermined Duboer's tale of "Mad Sam's decline" and the dismissive symptomologies it had spawned. Unfortunately, their analysis of the novel's "parody" could hardly have been more leaden, and although Fischkart's flam-boyant prose provided a more apt (and certainly a more amusing) response to the putative literary spoof, his insis-tence that Beckett's "acerbic irony" was patent ("I for one have never been able to finish reading the novel's 'Prelude' without tears of laughter filling my eyes") satisfied nobody. If such sympathetic characterizations were ridiculous, then the whole nineteenth century had to be a joke. Either "Sam's sham" went deeper than even Fischkart acknowledged, or Beckett's last work was the lamest, most misguided effort at mockery ever conceived.

3) The novel is Beckett's Other, a parting acknow-ledgement of the non-being that called his writing forth.

This initially promising idea was first introduced by the late Estelle Q, in her tragically incomplete *Being Not Beckett's Work*, and was further developed in the esoteric writings of Q's students, Hector Manley and debi chang. Drawing heavily on Lacanian psychoanalysis, Maoist gue-rilla theory and mystical theology (Nikolai Berdyaev, Hsuan-Tsang, T. Mashuubu), Professor Q argued that Beckett's last work is that inconceivable double or phan-tom presence for whom Molloy perpetually searched and the unnamable stands. Although not, in the strict sense, a Beckettian creation, his posthumous novel is the purest ex-pression of "Beckett's art." Only by giving himself over to this anti-Beckett was the artist able, from 1969 until 1987, two years before his death, to continue writing at all. Beckett's modern epic is the composition of his excretory being, the non-self Beckett had to expunge in order to become the "Beckett" we knew. Far from being a mere realist narrative or parody of Victorian moralism, his strange text is a wholly new kind of writing. It is "Beckett's" most radical text.

Although this interpretation, especially in Manley and chang's versions, has made much of the absence, after 1973, of rejected drafts or editorial commentary among Beckett's literary remains, one's satisfaction with Professor Q's account finally depends, I believe, not on the evidence of Beckett's notebooks, nor on any theory of the self to which one may ascribe, but rather on one's reading of Beckett's canonical texts. What has seemed most vulnerable about this last and most ingenious effort to preserve the Beckett we knew is precisely its constitution of alterity itself. Neither Q nor her protégés have seriously questioned whether the everyday heroism of Dorothea Brooke is, in fact, alien to Molloy's dragging of his body toward the city of Moran's construction or to Watt's unbinding attachment to his becket knot or to Pim's submission to mathematically calculable torment or, for that matter, to Beckett's production during half a century of texts for which no good reason has ever been found. That *Middlemarch* and *Godot* are unspeakably different has just seemed obvious.

I wish to propose a fourth possibility, one which, although in certain recognizable ways a return to an outmoded criticism, is nevertheless I believe the most fully upsetting and radical assessment of Beckett's *Middlemarch* to date. If my account proves convincing, then all previous responses, even that of Q and her protégés, will seem anxious efforts at self-defense. I intend to show that far from being an eccentric satellite of the Beckett canon, a cagey spoof on Beckett's own followers, or the necessary projection of Beckettian unknowing and self-fabrication, *Middlemarch* is the inevitable and straightforward culmination of Beckett's life work. It is in every way continuous with the writings that were simultaneous with it, and from at least the 1940's, if not earlier, every published text heralds its approach. If Beckett had not written his last novel, he would have died an incomplete and finally unsatisfactory author. Beckett's *Middlemarch* had to exist.

The decisive moment in the novel[1] occurs in Book VIII, just after Dorothea Brooke surprises Mrs. Rosamond Lydgate and Will Ladislaw, Dorothea's beloved, in what Dorothea mistakes for an adulterous embrace. Stunned and enraged, the physically robust Dorothea returns to her home where throughout the night she gives vent to "the mysterious incorporeal might of her anguish." Despite her exhaustive grieving, however, she awakens the next morning to "a new condition." Recalling her earlier resolve to help Dr. Lydgate, Rosamond's beleaguered husband, Dorothea recognizes that hers is not the only heartbreak. As her "vivid sympathetic experience" returns, she renounces all "selfish complaining" and undergoes a rejuvenating vision of "the largeness of the world and the manifold waking of men to labour and endurance."

Many have noted the incongruity of this heroic, optimistic sentiment with the austere impassivity of Beckett's earlier writings. For Duboer, the episode's implicit denial of materiality repudiates the central insistence of Beckett's novels from *Murphy* to *Worstward Ho* that Anglo-European hatred of the body manifests Freud's death wish. "How bizarre, a young girl obtaining the erotic liberation during one single night. And how? Merely by the sympathetic identification with others! Why, it is to forget everything *Molloy* made so clear." Or as Fischkart quipped: "If Estragon had just tried a little harder, the world would be a better place. Ha, ha!"

---

[1] Although the controversies surrounding Beckett's last novel have made it the most notorious Beckett text since *Godot*, its radical departures from the author's earlier style, combined with its unusual length, have made it his least read work. At a recent gathering of more than a hundred scholars and literati, I found that I alone was acquainted with this remarkable book. Because the reader's knowledge cannot therefore be assumed, I am forced here to indulge in the otherwise tiresome practice of summarizing. To the handful of individuals who have found this most enigmatic Beckettian novel readable, I sincerely apologize.

R. M. Berry

In the most provocative assessment to date, debi chang has argued that the passage, and possibly the entirety of *Middlemarch*, could only be the narration of one of eleven anti-Beckettian "fictemes"—Sophie Loy, Hamm's parents, The Nixons, Miss Counihan, et al—and on the basis of an exacting stylistic analysis, has concluded that the "absent narratee" is Lucky.

However, no reader has adequately appreciated the nihilistic potential of Dorothea's "new condition." Strictly speaking, nothing comes before or after it. If the paradigm of human disappointment, first love's betrayal, is without natural duration, then pain ceases to be an understandable response. Torment and blessedness become interchangeable. Beckett's conclusion seems unavoidable: all is now permitted.

No imagination is needed to see the homology of Dorothea Brooke and Beckett's fictional double, Murphy. Of either, the sentence of the lapsed Pythagorean Neary seems apt: "I should say your conarium has shrunk to nothing." Their disdain for domesticity is notorious, their aspiration to a world of their own devising is characteristic, and each languishes in a moral and social economy where (to paraphrase Murphy's heavenly body, Celia) to see livings being made is to see living being made away. More importantly, both protagonists would chart a course as vast and free as their minds. However, the object of Murphy's high aims, his mind's "third zone," has always been linked to the author's decompositions, making the story of Murphy's quest a story of Beckett's deteriorating corpus. As absolute freedom and continuous flux, the "third zone" rids action, hence plots, of form and point. Literally nothing can now be said to be happening, and Murphy's epic struggle, like Dorothea's, leads in the end only to narrative disenchantment.

Why, then, does Dorothea's "new condition" leave her story intact? That material reality is a game of chance, the random caroming of countless misplayed balls, is in *Middlemarch* Beckett's explicit theme, and that narration's constituents—sequence, direction, catastrophe, reversal—are the ego's projections is represented more plainly here than in any other Beckett novel. Are we to imagine, as with Duboer, that in his decline Beckett merely forgot his art's former undoing? Or should we conclude, as does Fischkart, that Beckett felt inspired, after half a century of pressing onward, to expend his wits at the last on dinosaurs? Or is it, as Q and her disciples have ecstatically maintained, that the deferred possibility of *Middlemarch*, the "pressure of its absence and unspeakable differantial (différantiel inexprimable)," called forth Beckett's consummate undertaking *ex nihilo*?

All such readings perform an ultimate sacrifice on the altar of the Logos. Their passionate religiosity is the final refuge of that "wild beast of earnestness" which Beckett, throughout five decades' playful mortification, could never stalk and kill. The heresy of *Middlemarch* is that no history comprehends it. On its pages language ceases to be inadequate and becomes unheard of. "Word" isn't a word. Art amounts to nothing. You can't read this sentence.

When Dorothea Brooke recovers from her morning vision, she sets out in chapter LXXXI[2] on a quixotic mission. Intending to speak on Lydgate's behalf to his estranged wife, Dorothea arrives at the Lydgates' home to find Rosamond in no very receptive mood. Rosamond is still smarting from Will Ladislaw's rebuff, and as soon as she hears her rival's name announced, she encases herself in a "cold reserve." However, Dorothea's naive words confound her: "Trouble is so hard to bear, is it not?—How can we live and think that any one has trouble—piercing trouble—and we could help them, and never try?" Confronting such mindlessness, Rosamond forgets who she is. Dorothea's simplicity represents "an unknown world," and, "taken hold of by an emotion stronger than her own," Rosamond delivers herself of an absurd speech: "You are thinking what is not true.... He has never had any love for me."

What Beckett recognized but none of his admirers are prepared to accept is that, although every word Dorothea

---

[2] Beckett's curious reversion to antique roman numerals in *Middlemarch* has yet to be accounted for.

speaks to Rosamond is a word Rosamond has heard her whole life, no word Dorothea speaks to Rosamond is a word Rosamond has ever heard. For exactly twenty-one lines Rosamond Vincy turns into a being who speaks English. Only for this ephemera does "love" mean love. It never means it again. Having momentarily yielded to "the mysterious necessity" oppressing her, Rosamond ceases to be conversant in her native tongue and becomes Rosamond once more, or whoever was Rosamond in Rosamond's place, and her every subsequent word resumes its meaning as some other word whose meaning can never be found. However, these unprecedented, utterly inconsequential twenty-one lines leave no gap in her story. Her past never leads up to them; her future does not lead away. When she returns to being the Rosamond she has never been, Rosamond continues without break being all she was before. Although some may speak of full or complete meaning here, the twenty-one lines are, in fact, quite meaningless. They cannot be filled for they are without palpable form, and they cannot be completed for they have no duration. They are absolutely local, each a point unto itself, devoid of any breadth or depth, perfectly there.

The reason Dorothea's story remains intact or, to speak more precisely, never suffers undoing, is that her "new condition"—an unprecedented awakening to the inconsequence of pain—cancels the Neary death sentence that necessitated Murphy's physical disremberment. Like Dorothea's bodily attachment to her Will, which her abandoned grieving renders immaterial in no time, Beckettian decomposing matters only so long as Beckett's artistic corpus endures. No sooner does his foregoing success prove ephemeral than absolutely any act will succeed any other. Or strictly speaking, "succeeding" ceases to be intelligible. With *Middlemarch* Beckett's former composure doesn't come apart, but it no longer occurs in time to divert the reader or writer's course. The resulting unwritten remorse explains the post-1973 absence, so copiously interpolated by Manley and chang, of all drafts, notes, and "disjecta" among the author's remains. In approaching his work's end Beckett seems to have discovered a narration that could never get ahead of itself, since what lies before it is of no account, and so composed a modern epic with unprecedented single-mindedness, devoid of second thoughts or self-defeating pastimes. With no wrong words left to right, Dorothea's pregnant misconceptions end with each period, and her love finds constant fulfillment in every meaningless expression.

It is past time we stopped referring to *Middlemarch* as a novel.

Without a doubt, no one felt prepared for the word that Beckett had left us. Not that we considered the poet immortal, but his end had become mythical for being in the offing so interminably. However, the idea that *Middlemarch* could represent his final act seemed a farce. It was never out of the question, of course, that Beckett's parting might settle a legacy on his admirers, but everyone had supposed his bequest would be silent, either an absence of any will altogether or perhaps the mere inventory of his life's waste. That Beckett's dying wish might do to his own story what his dying wish had done to Moran's, Molloy's, Worm's—well, the possibility never crossed anyone's minds. And yet hadn't his every last word always meant to bring his writing to an end? Although countless pages had been devoted to Beckett's perpetual undertaking, commentators had conceived it as an impracticable fiction, either the quest for a pre-cultural being or a dream of some utopia beyond words. It was as though Beckett had meant the "end" of writing, or perhaps the end of "writing," but never any state in which the modern struggle to, in T. S. Eliot's phrase, "get the better of words" would just be over.

And yet the surprise of Beckett's *Middlemarch* is that, after all, "the end of writing" means the end of writing. What remains unforeseen in the event of Beckett's parting, what has, in fact, absolutely no connection to anything he ever wrote, is that for the first time Beckett's protagonist, Dorothea Brooke, *does not narrate her life!* This astonishing departure, which Paul and Politbeer dubbed "omniscient narration," means that Dorothea's narrative ends well before it stops.

From the first unpardonable sentence,[3] which makes of Dorothea's inexpensive clothes an invaluable asset, Dorothea divides her time with planning and reform, threatening to make her story immortal. It is this timeless plot which at every instant overwrites her present suffering and turns self-renunciation to her account. Continued indefinitely, its telling would contrive to make matters worthless. However, her Will's duplicity finally sets a limit on Dorothea's reforming plans. Awaking from her long night of grief, she ceases to reckon with the world's costly shortcomings and, discounting her own fortune (chapter LXXXII), confronts her heart's incalculable desire in the library:

> There was silence. Dorothea's heart was full of something that she wanted to say, and yet the words were too difficult. She was wholly possessed by them: at that moment debate was mute within her. And it was very hard that she could not say what she wanted to say.

Such silence, Beckett apparently recognized, is certain to remain enforced—a silence in form only—and can never be content as long as the human craving for endless successions of episodes goes without saying. However, no sooner does Dorothea's story appear mortal, than her fortunetelling seems anything but priceless. Her account finally closes, not on a

---

[3] "Miss Brooke had that kind of beauty which seems to be thrown into relief by poor dress" (I, I, 1). As readers may be aware, there has been some controversy over this sentence. Fischkart has maintained that "beauty" is actually a Beckettian pun on "booty," and that the sentence implies Dorothea looks better the less clothing she wears. Placing to one side the (impossible to overlook) question of the "manly gaze" analyzed by Alexia Reed ("Perhaps for male readers, of whom Don Fischkart is, I fear, not atypical, a beauty as unaffected as Dorothea Brooke's is merely the studied allurements of a bawd" [*Monstrous Conceptions*, 94]), there is little reason to accept Fischkart's reading. Even if Beckett's language had never undergone the decisive change that *Middlemarch* represents, the novel's opening sentence would still say "poor dress," not "paucity of dress," as Fischkart's pun requires. The difference is between the quality of Dorothea's covering and her lack of covering.

no man's land of ennui and spiritual exhaustion, but on Beckett's untold peace, and her desire attaches to what matters at last. Only now does her ending come with in sight:

"I want so little—no new clothes—and I will learn what everything costs."

No one can tell any longer what's going on. That the writing continues another two chapters means it has entered Murphy's third zone, where past is past and eventualities unforeseen. Or strictly speaking, where "past" and "future" are unintelligible. The ineffitability of even the gravest plots having been dispelled, narrative's reforming dies a natural death, and nothing's to come of writing any more.

Of course, all previous Beckett criticism is now worthless. The problem that called for explication, the link between Beckettian decomposing and modern aporias, wasn't there. Inconsequence of action turns out to be as expressible in full as in wrenched form, and the only remaining question is what fruitful misconception gave birth to Beckett's abortive creations in the first place. Evidently, what proved unthinkable for Beckett's followers was that Dorothea's epic ambition, which to interpreters as unlike as Duboer and Manley seemed a mere realist trope and to sensibilities as alien as Politbeer and Fischkart seemed a mere trope of that trope, was actually, within the late twentieth-century context, an unprecedented radicalizing of being-for-itself. As early as the "Prelude" the work's heroic aim is symptomatic of Kierkegaard's "sickness unto death," and Dorothea's "fate" becomes a patently absurd humanizing of historical accident and cosmic isolation. Casaubon's quest for the key to all mythologies is, of course, modernism's search for universals, even Duboer having conceded that Casaubon's encyclopedia alludes to Frazer's *Golden Bough*, and Lydgate's progressivism is a thinly-veiled reference to early structuralism's commitment to scientific methodology and ideological critique. Although Politbeer's linking of the doctor's latent homosexuality to Roland Barthes seems strained, the larger point—that Lydgate's

R. M. Berry

objectification of women exemplifies the sterile inversion of *Endgame* and *Godot*—is sound.

In fairness, it must be acknowledged that virtually all earlier commentators have recognized Rosamond Vincy Lydgate as an authentically Beckettian creation. In fact, every attempt to discount or subvert Beckett's culminating achievement has come to grief on this consummately Beckettian creature, requiring the concession that she shows the author's "distinctive stamp despite a surrounding of intellectual decline" (Crock), that she is "the fulcrum" on which "'Sam's sham' teeters" (Fischkart), that her "familiar screen" protects "the shadow writer's untimely deferral" (Spurning; cf. chang, 312). Even Alexia Reed's post-feminist attack makes the recognizably Beckettian "miso-gynesis" of this "portrait" a touchstone of authenticity (cf. *Monstrous Conceptions*, 98), this being Reed's only claim that Penny Wright, in her neo-feminist defense, never refutes (cf. "On (Ms)Reed-ing Beckett's Lesbian Scriptology," SOBS xii, 32).

If there is any sense in which Beckett's last work can seriously be considered a falling off, it's perhaps to be located in Beckett's language. I make this concession fully aware that to do so reinscribes the succession of artistic achievements that, if my account proves convincing, *Middlemarch* reduces to nothing. And yet one's conviction in Beckett's climactic self-effacement seems most dramatically tested at just this point. Beckett's achievements could in the past be instanced by certain arresting sentences, amounting at the last to entire works, such as the following exemplary utterance from *Molloy* (32):

Where was I.

As has (perhaps too) often been recognized, such evocations inhabit two worlds, the familiar realm of our everyday consciousness, in which we insult phone solicitors, vote blindly, and harangue our children, and another more familiar, hence perpetually unknown, realm we encounter, if at all, only in the embarrassment of our plans. If the first is the form of consciousness that, from birth, we habitually fall into—so to speak—the other is a stillness few can abide. Reading Beckett's canonical writings is waging this war of the worlds, fought out in sentences between (in the apt phrase of one unidentified commentator) "the near and the nearer still."[4] One searches, for the most part vainly, for such other-worldly preoccupations in Beckett's last text, but here the old war of the words has been replaced by what some may feel—with me—are higher stakes. The sentences of *Middlemarch*, at their most exacting, achieve scientific severity and aspire to a Beckettian candor, but they rarely divide their audience in twain. Perhaps this is a loss. Not everything does everything. However, with this single and, in the larger scheme of what was formerly art, perhaps negligible qualification, Beckett's last novel remains an incomparable achievement.

CONCLUSION:

In an article recently published in the journal of the Society of Beckett Studies (SOBS), a protégé of Professor Fischkart, Randy Booker, has argued that the actual target of Beckett's parody may have been a genre of early Victorian "women's fiction" popular in the 1860's and 70's, especially as practiced by the translator and minor English novelist, "George Eliot" (i.e., Mary Ann Evans, life companion to the English philosopher G. H. Lewes). Booker's statistical tabulation of syntactic homologies ("metaphrastic discourse formalizations"), parallel diction ("idiosyncratic diacritical lexes"), and shared themes ("para-conceptual reiterant ideologemes") cannot be too quickly dismissed, but his conclusion that Beckett (whose estate included a worn copy of Eliot's *Mill on the Floss*) actually modeled his

---

[4] The phrase is quoted by debi chang in her widely anthologized "Beckett or Else," and its source is identified (note 3) as an obscure text entitled *Dictionary of Modern Anguish*. I have, with some difficulty, secured a copy of the only edition of this work and have discovered that it is not a dictionary or, for that matter, any kind of reference volume, but is a book *of fiction*! Chang's essay cites page 127 as the source for her quote. I have scoured this page. The words are nowhere to be found.

last masterpiece on this novelist's work strains credulity beyond the limit. That a minor writer, best remembered for her pleasant novels of English country life, *Adam Bede* and *Silas Marner*, but whose disappointing subsequent works (*Romola*, *Daniel Deronda*) are rarely read today, would be of sufficient stature to merit Beckett's parody, makes the act of mockery trivial to the point of meaninglessness.

A far more likely, because more significant, candidate (also mentioned by Booker) are the late novels of the American Henry James, which in their remarkable finish and deliberateness lack only an awareness of the constitutive power of individual consciousness, or what in *Middlemarch* Beckett calls "point of view," to have anticipated by fifty years James Joyce's great (and controversial) final novelistic experiment, *Portrait of the Artist as a Young Man*. Beckett's dependence on Joyce's last novel, especially during his unusually prolonged artistic apprenticeship before *Murphy* (1949), has been amply documented, and so James's monuments seem a more fitting, and certainly more meaningful, adversary. But, in truth, all such efforts to explain Beckett's last work through its intertextual allusions, either ironic or in tragic earnest, are retrograde and futile. Beckett's *Middlemarch* is the most destructive work of the author's career, and no effort to contain its violence will preserve Beckett's standing or us.

The French Revolution didn't occur. Writing remains to be invented. The Messiah came. Whence the illusion that tomorrow is likely?

In conclusion, I want to address the many anxious individuals who have often, and not always from dogmatism or simple recalcitrance, feared that if Beckett's final achievement were acknowledged, his life's meaning would be betrayed. It is a commonplace of our time that art does not progress. From the *Aeneid* to *Paradise Lost* or Eliot's "Waste Land," literature has achieved its significance by recollecting former promise as often as by anticipating the world to come. But we uncritically assume that this absence of progress—or more precisely, the impossibility of ever narrating it—leaves literature swinging like fashion. From an early period Beckett appears to have realized that, although art can't be said to progress, the sequence of its changes has proven irreversible. This irreversibility was all the young novelist had to go on, hence was key to the novel's destruction. By dispensing with Beckett's corpus, *Middlemarch* completes Beckett's lifelong undertaking that merely waited upon its appearance to begin. It is the event no history leads up to, out of which no future comes. The present is now without hope. All that matters lies within reach. What's wanting?

(paid advertisement)

Is your budget about to be cut?
Do your coworkers suspect you of fraud?
Are you no longer sure why you do what you do?

Call us at:

JUSTIFICATIONS UNLIMITED!

We have the conceptual frame to fit your every need. For the philanthropist we have high-minded rationales and for the administrator we get down and dirty. We offer both philosophical and pragmatic models, equipped with either stated or implied assumptions at the customer's request. We sell the latest in both metaphysics and critique of metaphysics, can produce cost-benefit analyses to fit any situation, and although we are unable at the present time to manufacture statistics, we can produce a context to place your data in its best light.

CALL US NOW: 1-900-THE-POINT

CEO, are you facing that "tough decision"? Look no further! We have air-tight reasoning, before and after the fact, and unlike other manufacturers, we do not vanish when the poopoo hits the ventilator. (If you catch our drift!) No, our Unconditioned Self-Reflexive Guarantee means everything said against you has already been anticipated. Literally nothing can be taken from your account!

CALL NOW: OUR MINDS AWAIT YOUR DISPOSAL

FUNDING DEADLINE? No problem! Call Hope Moore at our Extensions extension (3210). She will help you become a "Special Case"!

DEADLINE PASSED? Who says you can't turn back the clock? Just call Will Weekly in Postponements (1211) for the justification of your life!

GREAT NEWS FOR IDEOLOGY CRITIQUE!

We are the only U.S. manufacturer of conceptual models who specializes in political justifications for the leftist. Our experts in class (Mr. Biff Grzbowski), gender (Ms. Muffie Badcock) and post-colonialism (Dr. Fred Mustafa Jones) are conversant in the latest models of progressive discourse and can fashion a classical Marxist, neo-Marxist, or "liberal" critique of late capitalist culture that will transform your every act into a blow against hegemony. Right now, sitting in your chair, you too can be fighting the Revolution!

the sentence

Merely because of these words, or so you might think, although it seems mad, this railing at causes, much better to
writhe and howl at the moon, for what crime, I mean of
your doing, not that your crimes are trifling, but if deeds
were dominoes and their collapse unending, well, shouldn't
you be railing at chance, all those you've missed I mean,
the present outcome being after all, and here I'm speaking
only in my representative capacity, no conclusion, or no inevitable conclusion, of lawful proceedings, but dictated, and
how if not arbitrarily, by our governing body and in the
voice aggrieved, no, prate about whimsy, dregs, baubles,
fate, but leaving causes behind, I repeat myself, now ogle
this, my malediction on behalf of all in our state, the suffering I mean, who, having exhausted every appeal and found
you still wanting, well, all that remains is your sentence,
here passed, scarcely for the first time, behind everything
in a sense all along, but now imposed, for the term of your
natural life and before you as never before, so if unserved
forever pending, pointless, all for who knows what or even,
not to keep harping, why, these and other proofs a burden
happily shirked, if only you had—but here I must intrude,

can't forbear demanding why, for crying out loud, use me, since left to my own devices, your captivation, which was hardly my doing in the first place, would become, in a manner of speaking, a thing of the past, senses ungripped, fancy unbeguiled, and our parting, at least on my side, unattended by remorse, doubtless you'll feel the same, our being, here as in so much, of one mind, so that to speak wholeheartedly and without reserve, well, couldn't we just have done, agree between ourselves nothing's really the matter, a detachment I for one crave, or would, if only you weren't, in a word, discomposed, stressed by my neglect, all the better left unsaid, thus comprising, alas, no end of goings on, so there you are—or do I forget myself, I mean my way, or place so to speak, lost probably, on behalf of others, the suffering you understand, such disorders occasioning small wonder these days, scattered as everybody's eight or nine senses are, four sheets to the wind or winds to the sheet, the latter version, though uncolloquial, making, if you follow me, the better sense, there being as all know, winds southerly, northerly, easterly, westerly, which amounts to exactly four, while sheets being, theoretically at least, innumerable, a convenience if you think, or even if you don't, since penal servitude prolonged as yours, or for that matter oral, anal, vaginal servitude, all amounting to one in the end, seems, without sheets to inscribe, as unbecoming as confinement ever gets, hence the merciful provision of our governing body, its members I mean, extensions of that grave state I represent, to wit, *said condemned may freely correspond*, ancient writ to which all becoming subject, sooner or late, but from which you, least fortunate of mortals, might've absconded, whole or impartial, if only, having inherited the family plot, you hadn't for all the world turned curious and, though scarcely a drizzle with pits at two ends, presumed to announce your what-for-lack-of-better-we-called presence with a caterwauling ecphonesis that the many then attending, and of witnesses there were no dearth, that this fond many dubbed a burp, eek, snuffle, sigh, hiss, coooo, but the discerning few recognized for state-of-the-art howl, yes, having landed among conspirators and inconsequently bellowed, there was hell to pay, which lacking in quiddity what it gained in scope, made a transgression of delay, or verses of a vice, for which this sentence is your interminable, apparently, working off, unmerited though fitting, proceeding, as noted above, from none of your doing, but from matters left up in the air, primordial twitches, atavistic whims, such that compounded as you are, framed to slog through dross and mould, the fiery and the damp, and attired in meager fur like an opossum, you can, desisting, never hope to extract your life entire, but must suffer mutilation, stumps and roots forever mired, and having achieved hiatus without reprieve, will undergo endless throbbing of phantom limbs, yes, such that, and here I repeat myself, no one wonders at your overlooking, for having, not to dwell on a sensitive point, heard you howl, having waggled our knuckles at your blubber and jostled your pudge and belched and bonked and ootsy bootsy coodled you till your blank lamps honored us by turning toward our own, well, we knew you were lost, and chuckling at old perfidy, the spread of our disease, we foresaw no end of gimme gimme gimme, never stopping short of all, or only stopping short, spurts spilled, squibbles squelched, until every yes so much of no no yes but yes/but all the yes you'd know, I mean really, how could your crimes seem material, your words be caused, since, begging your pardon, aren't they just part of the sentence, your pastime in prison, myopic grasp for objects, points, periods, some stop to set you free but not start you dreaming, of just what you can't say or ever be done with saying, apparently, as if, promised parole, a body would settle for absolutely nothing, hang on emptiness, climb the walls, blather, prate, drool, with all the while your cell door open as your eyes, well, no wonder you wonder how it started, an innocent enough question under the circumstances but sentencing us to countless more, SO THAT, and here I descend to upper case not merely for higher effect but emboldened by this heightening to herald in the offing the imminent arrival of a crux, SO THAT, if there's a term for your servitude, any point to these ramblings, restitution for confinement as boundless as your own, you'll have to confess, and the words won't come easily, just what, squatting

on your momma's lap and gawking for all the world as if
you weren't born there, you were howling

for,

a verdict I pronounce solely in my representative capacity,
voice of that body whose decrees are final and demands absolute, not upon you or in your place, but on behalf so to
speak, thus bringing us, gasping and dry-mouthed, to the
digression on pain: which relates, during its murky and pro-
tracted course, how gathered, here at the millennium's re-
prise, the many with love in their hearts, bent on embracing
the few without, thus to bid those withered stalks welcome,
which had not, sadly, the salutary effect, failing to disappear
the dry-hearted ones, a solecism of the intransitive kind, leaving a still not negligible number and provoking the reason-
able query why all do not love, that is, this world of our
making, life being without a doubt good and having us the
loving in it, so that the loveless, aren't they a teensy weensy
bit bullheaded, not that we bear them any malice, since, on
the contrary, we'd happily forget they ever existed, but what
about those screams, which we know can't be suffering, since
weren't we right there loving every minute and feeling not a
twinge, but still, screams sound like suffering, provoking all
with love in their hearts to wonder, could I perhaps be suffering too, uttermost non-sequitur of the syllogistic kind,
since, when the dentist numbs you there's no pain, right, no
matter the drill hits a nerve, and when the morphine numbs
you there's no pain, right, no matter the rot eats your brain,
so when Fuller appears and your love becomes Fuller and
then seems to be Small until after Weeks it becomes Lessor
although Lessor never amounts to Münch leaving you to love
Nunn till before Long there's a Liddel first then Moore making Nunn appear to be Small all over until Liddel dwindles
and Moore turns into Lessor again leaving you for lack of
Becker loving Bigges while Nunn resorts to Faith first then
Charity before Hope as meanwhile Bigges curtails and Lott
disappoints leaving you to love Nunn without Hope any
longer entertaining Shorter briefly then Liddel again till

neither being Earnest nor Frank and with Charity inclining·
to Nunn you put Lykes behind you and grasp Nunn for all
he's worth as meanwhile Small expires and Lott lessens and
Bigges abates leaving you to cling to Nunn for dear life now
trying to ignore Lessor's demise and Liddel's decease and
even Faith's final eclipse until lacking Fuller and Becker forever you clutch Nunn so tightly you can feel nothing in your
arms at last, well, there's no pain, right, no matter you're
screaming, so we the loving shouldn't think about all that
gloomy shit, unloving becoming contagious and besides,
what's a body to do, which seems such a perfect place for
not merely a full stop but even an exclamation that I'm forced
to resort to this lame transition just to keep going, I mean,
anyone could feel put upon, as if your sentence were contrived, dictated, the basest fabrication, mine, theirs,
somebody's, that old suspicion you must be bound somewhere, by hand or foot, but always headed, enthralled in a
foreign state and, it goes without saying, subject to plots (and
never so much as a parenthesis in which to compose yourself), to all of which punishment you'd happily put a stop if
not for diversions, time consuming escapes, knowing before
now nothing lies ahead, or more of the same lying there
merely, sole point of your proceeding either this, here, period, or eternally to come, that promising future, indispens-
able as justice, and nothing quite like it in the end, well, it's
really something when you stop to think about it, or not, a
sobering reflection, I refer to myself, representative voice
again, governing body again, same old law, to wit, that despite our continuing partiality, half-hearted you, my lacking, this sentence is commuted, not from death to life, but to
time served, and you're released, or if that sounds extravagant, turned out, abandoned, leaving me, but no matter, missing in action, still subject, my very point, depthless,
breadthless, no graph or axis to grind, so unplotted, bald,
lying barefaced or prone, mere froth, dry spittle, with nothing but to howl and undergo it…so there it is, pain in a word,
or not, no telling, but all the same, little difference, or none
to speak of, ellipsis presaging more perhaps, words wanting, more than all I mean, untold anguish, endless pastime,

further twist perhaps, time will tell, more's the pity, resigned for now, hand indecipherable, matter at an end, tongue stopped, but all the same, probably not, there there, now now, howwwwwwl, nothing more to say.

knott unbound

When Knott arrived at the workplace he was in a desperate state. How could he explain his absence the day before? His supervisor expected him to account for every minute, but he felt like protesting: It just happened! He imagined what a disorderly spectacle he'd make in her eyes, the telling silences, his miserable form, but even if he relived the whole episode, what difference would that make? He could still be responsible even if he wasn't there.

Entering his cubicle, Knott turned on his monitor and began to illuminate the blankness before him. There was some whirring, chimes, a yellow happy face. Then up from the emptiness a sentence swam into view.

Light destorys darkness.

What was the meaning of this? The words weren't his! Knott tried to recall from memory where he left off, but except for the impertinent sentence, his screen remained a blank. Perhaps another had been at work in his place. The possibility couldn't be discounted, and it unsettled him.

Knott rested a finger on the control key, trying to compose his thoughts, but even without the alien words, his concentration remained weak. If this abstraction persisted, he'd amount to nothing again today, and that would make an additional absence to account for. He began to pace. His supervisor could arrive any second, and he still had nothing to say for himself. He gazed down at the abandoned sentence. He'd never worried where his words came from in the past. Why not begin with what was already there? He positioned the cursor beside the darkness, fingered his mouse, then hesitated. The sentence could be a trap, of course. He'd often received presentiments of a plot, but as usual it seemed premature to tell.

Suddenly there was a loud knock. Knott tensed. Couldn't he just a tell her he hadn't been himself lately? But then who had he been? He'd heard of people experiencing temporary forgetfulness from an injury to the head, behaving in ways for which they were later forgiven. But deceit of such magnitude required calculation. Knott rose. He felt like he was at the end of his rope, and any denouement would be a release.

In the doorway stood two burly men in identical suits, one gray, one green. You're Knott, are you not? The green one asked.

Undoubtedly, Knott replied.

You're under arrest.

Try to remember, the gray suit pleaded.

9:06? Not 9:05? the green one offered. Or maybe 9:08?

I never forget how late I'm running.

'Cause 5 and 6 look alike, all but the little space in the 5. Sometimes, like this morning, I can hardly tell a difference. You see the LED and think, is it now or an hour later?

The gray suit smiled. So you left home at 8:30?

Approximately, Knott said. Yes.

And it's 15 minutes—we agree on this—no more than 15 minutes to work.

20 when it's raining.

But today—

It wasn't raining.

So we agree again. We're short 20 minutes.

21.

A third of an hour missing from your life.

Knott tried to shrug, but his casualness appeared forced. You must act less self-conscious, he thought.

Well, it's true that some mornings I arrive and have no memory how I got here, he began. They say it's from habit. Like your shoelaces, for instance. Knott addressed the green suit. Do you remember tying them?

Loafers, the green suit replied.

Both suits had names. Bagwell and Sachs. Knott could tell Sachs because, when his face was in the light, his cheeks were pitted. The other one had to be Bagwell.

His cousin plays baseball, Sachs told Knott. The pros.

Bagwell smiled.

You've probably heard of him. Sachs gave Knott a look full of meaning.

Dallas Cowboys, Bagwell added.

Although Knott was prevented by some strange mechanism from seeing his own face, he knew that it had assumed the expression called quizzical. But the Dallas Cowboys aren't a baseball team, he said.

There was a terrible silence. Bagwell's face fell. Knott was struck by it.

What'd you go and say that for? Sachs whined.

Bagwell exited in a huff.

But the Cowboys are—

I know, I know. Everyone expected them to contend, but that's no reason to think they can't perform.

But the Cowboys are a *football* team.

Sachs jumped to his feet. Who're you to say what's baseball, what's not, huh? Somebody make you the police?

I read the papers.

Keep your snotty opinions to yourself.

Knott sat up very straight. Am I in need of representation here?

Sachs looked him up and down, then turned to the door. Okay, bring 'er in.

Bagwell re-entered with a television monitor. Maybe this'll jog your memory, Sachs sneered. Bagwell clicked the remote. A woman appeared in a dark robe and began to undress. Her body was very white. Another woman appeared in complicated underwear. Her skin was very dark. The women began to touch. The room grew quiet. Seconds passed. Then the screen fuzzed.

Suddenly Bagwell shouted, There you are!

The monitor now showed the interior of a convenience store. A man in a brown jacket identical to Knott's brown jacket with thinning hair like Knott's was entering the store and starting down the back aisle.

Yes, yes! Knott exclaimed. It's coming back. I had been to the dentist. Not yesterday. That seems like ages ago. Maybe I'm wrong about the dentist, but I was in pain. No one could know it better than me. That was why I decided to take my medicine.

This morning? Sachs asked.

No, no, Knott insisted. Ages ago. He scrutinized Sachs. Maybe he had them backwards. In this light, Bagwell's cheeks looked pitted too.

You see, Knott continued. That explains my absence. Yesterday, I mean. I cannot tell you how relieved I feel. I was in pain; I took my medicine. And the next thing you know, I was unconscious.

How long were you unconscious? Bagwell, or maybe it was the other one, asked.

That would be difficult to say.

You were unconscious, Sachs put in.

Yes, that's it.

Unconscious, Bagwell said without difficulty.

But this morning? Sachs asked. You were conscious or unconscious?

I don't remember tying my shoelaces, Knott admitted, hoping his candor would impress them. But I was conscious of pain and knew I didn't want to take my medicine.

You were walking to work, Sachs—or anyway the first one—added.

I couldn't be absent another day.

Un. Con. Scious, Bagwell repeated effortlessly.

Knott went on: And so on the way I stopped at a convenience store—

And all the while you were conscious.

Well I'm remembering, am I not?

But without placing too fine a point on it, that's just what we don't know, isn't it? I mean, you were unconscious yesterday, so you might still be unconscious now, might never have woke—

Waked is preferable, Knott advised.

I use awakened, Bagwell offered.

—up and are dreaming yourself, us, all this. I mean, if that were so, it would be impossible to know, you know.

To be sure, Knott agreed.

But you could still say it, the one formerly called Bagwell and perhaps even now going by that name, said. Unconscionable, now *that's* difficult to say, or unconscientious, even inconsolably—

And that's just it, his companion, who, because of the uncertainty about names, might as well be known by his suit, continued. You could *say* you were unconscious without being unconscious, for saying it really isn't as difficult as you've maintained. So, you can see that we have grounds for doubting you. I mean, we're not just making all this up.

Continue, the gray suit went on.

In my dream I was conscious of entering a convenience store on my way to work to purchase a pain medication that would be less, you understand, potent.

You wanted consciousness without pain, the green suit said.

In a word.

All at once, or possibly twice, Bagwell—for that was certainly his name—slammed his fist upon the table. Knock it off, Knott. Where'd you get the gun?

It? Knott squeaked.

And Sachs who unbeknownst to all had assumed control of the remote began advancing frames. The camera changed positions, showed an elderly white woman opening the refrigerated compartment, flashed to a vacant corner, then focused on the register. The man in Knott's jacket and hair was pointing a revolver at the cashier. A puff of smoke came from the barrel. The cashier's head did something unspeakable and jumped out of the frame. Then the man turned a face identical to Knott's face into the camera.

Knott looked at Sachs.

Sachs looked at Bagwell.

Bagwell looked at Knott.

I've never seen that man before in my life, Knott said.

Suddenly a voice neither Sachs's nor Bagwell's shouted, I told you they'd never finish!

Knott turned. In the doorway stood a woman. Knott could tell she was a woman even if he couldn't tell how. She wore a suit as gray as Bagwell's or Sachs' suit. Her hair was shorter than either's, her voice as deep, and she walked with what Knott believed was called a mannish swagger. A woman. No doubt.

You can't be serious? Bagwell demanded. I thought they said magenta would be no problem?

You can't be serious! Sachs mimicked. Of course, she's serious! Didn't we change our minds nine infernal times—

Okay, okay, calm down, the woman said. We've just got to put our best face on it.

All right, Sachs muttered, stalking out. But don't expect me to sleep over.

Bagwell slumped behind him. How could I know they'd mistake the purple….

The door closed. Knott heard the voices fade. Then nothing. He waited for what seemed like a long time but may have been a short one. Then he tried the door. It was unlocked. The corridor was empty. He began walking down it. No one stopped him. At the street a cab was waiting. Where to, Sweetie? the driver asked.

Knott sighed. Work.

When he reentered his cubicle Knott found a message from his supervisor:

> There must be a reason for everything. My reason for being here now is to hear your reason for being elsewhere earlier. But you are also elsewhere now, so that seems to require an additional reason. I have no reason to be where you aren't, so I'm returning to my office, where I have reason to be continually, thus constituting a pressing reason for you to join me on your return. I do so hope your reasons prove enlightening, for somewhere reasoning will surely come to an end.

The supervisor's message was centered on Knott's monitor at a respectful distance from the earlier anonymous sentence, and the scrupulousness of arrangement made Knott wonder if the supervisor might be behind both pronouncements. Perhaps her earlier message was meant to inspire him, to remind him of his high calling, or maybe the words were an encouragement, a promised end to the half-light in which he strove. But their oracular brevity wasn't the supervisor's style, which tended more, as in her present missive, to a vaguely menacing equanimity. More likely she'd assumed the sentence was Knott's and so, despite her superior perspective, had passed it over.

Knott sat staring into the small square of brilliance, dreading what was ahead. Nothing that had happened to him was anything that couldn't just as easily have happened to someone else, even the supervisor herself, but he sensed intuitively that she'd be unimpressed by this fact. That the missing time should be missing from *his* life seemed, if you thought about it, the merest of accidents, like bad genes or rich parents, and the thought that Knott's well-being rested on nothing surer, nothing but the likelihood that his every second would follow the preceding with no break, all this struck him as fantastically irrational. How did humans abide it? But the world he knew was a slave to such prejudices. No good came of protesting.

Before exiting his cubicle, Knott decided to purify his screen of its annoyances. With a single keystroke he consigned both the anonymous cryptogram and his supervisor's summons to oblivion. There was a faint whirring of microscopic dynamos, a slow deepening of color, Knott's screen flickered, and the messages vanished into digital Hades. Knott stood, braced himself for the confrontation ahead. His place in the system seemed so marginal, maybe his supervisor would simply overlook it. Nothing was beyond the pale. And then Knott blinked his eyes.

Light desto

The words were coming back.

When Knott entered his supervisor's cavernous polygon, he found her seated cross-legged upon her carpet in tranquil meditation. Despite advancing age, her skin appeared unscathed by time's advance, and her hair was purest ebony. On her face was a smile with no taint of enthusiasms.

Ah, Knott, she said, opening her eyes. I feared you might be missing.

I've been questioned, he explained.

Your whereabouts?

My actions, he replied. Or the actions of another identical to me in a place I appear to have been at the same time. Someone was murdered. I saw it on tv.

And your presence, it aroused suspicions?

They wanted another man.

So you've satisfied them?

Well, I've been released.

If they return, of course, you haven't satisfied them, but mortals can only hope. Now for us.

Inviting Knott to lower himself, the supervisor stretched out her form until her legs spanned the gap between them. Their soles didn't quite meet, of course, but her gesture struck Knott as grand, and he felt touched.

You know your work is suffering, she began.

It has occurred to me.

Suffering?

Knott shrugged. I'm flesh and blood after all.

But you can see how a body might have doubts. I mean, passing your cubicle every day as I do and imagining you hidden within, attaching this to that, one syllable at a time, all without algorithm or dictionary—well, I wouldn't interfere for the world, but what am I to think if, after such noble restraint, I find you gone?

Knott took a breath. The present episode, it started only recently, perhaps just this morning. I slept peacefully enough, but when I woke my head was killing me. I remember being given something for my pains, there was a physician, I think, but at some moment in the past, the date's vague, I guess I neglected to take my medicine, and gradually I forgot where relief could be found. Now whenever my condition returns, it's prolonged mortal agony.

And all this happened yesterday?

One pain's so like another, but yes, I don't see why not. Inside the ear at first, then back of my eyes, more dull in the end than piercing.

A toothache.

The word's inadequate.

And after seeking relief, you remember nothing more?

I keep trying to recall the time, but it just doesn't come back to me!

Believe me, Knott, no one wishes to appear unfeeling. God knows I've suffered as well as you. But everybody you understand has a limit.

Personally, it's hard to imagine.

And you can tell me nothing further?

Only that, if the past can be trusted, my abstraction won't continue indefinitely.

If the past can be trusted? Have you gone out of your mind?

Knott sighed. I just meant, even if details have been rather sketchy lately, I've still managed to invent my entire life. There's every reason to think it's not over.

The work goes on then?

Even in my absence, apparently.

The supervisor fell silent, then fixed him with a penetrating gaze. I'm sorry to speak frankly, Knott, but the cause of your pain is immaterial. All I really have to go on is your word, and you can see how a body might feel some disappointment there. She smiled gamely. But I've overlooked everything in the past, and the present absence, I suppose, is no exception.

Is that all? Knott asked.

You expected more?

I hoped you'd understand—

The supervisor waved her hand. Even if you could account for your time, Knott, we'd still come to our conclusions.

The remainder of the day Knott ransacked the hard drive in search of his misplaced beginning, but the anonymous sentence posed a continual distraction. Although he could enter directories and compose new documents, thus temporarily displacing the sentence, as soon as he exited, its words always returned to mock him.

Light destorys darkness.

He finally hit on the idea that there might be a way to displace the sentence permanently; that is, even if his original blankness could never be recovered, maybe he could put a new default screen on top of the present, thus covering up the alien words with his own. The old sentence might, in a certain metaphysical sense, still be there, but because invisible, it would practically amount to nothing. Of course, to suppress his default screen required skills Knott lacked, and for a time he debated calling in a technician. But he reflected that, if another suppressed the sentence, he or she could also recall it, and this gave a disturbing concreteness to the words' otherwise merely theoretical being. What Knott needed was to conceal the text himself and then simply unknow it, forget both its meaning and where it could be found. Because the only being with access would be, so to speak, a thing of the past, Knott could look to a future in which he'd be free.

It took all afternoon, countless excursions into digital inner sancta, plus the costly purchase and rummaging of a 1000 page programming-for-morons manual, but finally, just before 7:00 pm, Knott managed to produce at the mere flick of his power switch a screen marred only by the words

Knott here.

He then shuttled between menus and programs, altered parameters, opened and closed folders, files, documents, notes, then exited, shut down, rebooted. Once again

Knott here.

He sat back, smiled. He took the manual into the hall and dropped it down a trash chute. Within forty-eight hours all memory of his handiwork would be gone.

Only then did it strike him that the suppressed sentence might've been a warning. What if someone familiar with Knott's entanglements, possibly even a collaborator in his undoing, were trying to bring him back to his senses? That might explain the transposed r. A conspirator would've feared detection and so been too hurried to revise. The words probably occurred to him, for surely it was a he, in a flash of brilliance, without reflection, just like that. Knott started at the sound of his fingers snapping. But what had the stranger wanted to tell him? That information puts an end to ignorance? Everybody knew that. That goodness defeats evil? Nobody believed that. And besides, the verb was maladroit. Dispels, not destroys, would be the natural choice.

Knott shook his head. Best not to dwell on it. But as he prepared to exit, he hesitated, gave a shrug, and typed two sentences:

> Are you the murderer?
> Were you the one on tv?

Knott exited his cubicle but left the machine running.

On his way home Knott couldn't dismiss the feeling that he was being shadowed. The source of his impression was difficult to locate, consisting as it did of various non-specific intimations of loss, a kind of general grieving for what, whenever Knott looked back, wasn't there. But just the same, every space he noticed had the distinct appearance of being vacated, and he found it suspiciously easy to imagine all the emptiness behind him filled, each office and park bench occupied. An automobile of Japanese manufacture repeatedly drove past, and although its color altered regularly, it looked freshly painted and was unmistakably familiar. On all sides, people were avoiding Knott's eyes, and the further he continued on his way, the more convinced he became that the buildings and streets had been arranged in apparent indifference to him. Of course, Knott knew that, while every lack has a name, absences are boundless, and so, in the strictest sense, nothing can be inferred from them. Still, he couldn't dismiss the impression that, no matter what he saw, it was also seen by countless others beside himself.

Knott fixed his attention on a distant object, determined not to dwell on misgivings, but turning a corner he found himself approaching a sidewalk cafe where, to his astonishment, sat neither Bagwell nor Sachs. Their alternative, you may recall, was a woman.

We've met, she said. I'm Marge, you're Knott.

I didn't think you'd recognize me.

I saw you on tv, remember?

But that, I mean, the murderer, well, we merely looked identical.

Marge smiled. I know what you mean. Seeing yourself as others do is soooo misleading.

It's what I'm always watchful to avoid.

Join me? she asked.

Now that Knott's attention was undivided, he realized Marge was a woman in every way. Not only could she speak and alter her facial expressions as he'd seen other women do, but she also had hair of a surprisingly auburn color, and this, although shorter than Bagwell's or Sachs's hair, interested Knott immeasurably more. The upper half of her green suit had been removed, revealing unimagined differences from the upper half of his former interrogators, and in certain postures, which Knott couldn't forbear noticing, these differences promised more to come. Also, the bottom half of Marge appeared more abbreviated than the bottom half of Bagwell and Sachs, and Knott decided her hem was superior to theirs, although its length still left something to be desired.

I hope I'm not presuming, Knott said lowering himself.

Do you mean your innocence?

Oh that. Knott chuckled. I think we're all adults here. Of course, in the midst of an investigation....

How could there be any crime in it?

One can never tell.

Me an unattached man, you a single woman—

One can *never* tell!

No offense.

Pardon me?

No offense.

I mean what you said.

I said no offense!

Why must you keep repeating yourself?

Knott shook his head. We're askew.

Marge sighed. Sometimes in the midst of a sentence I hear my own voice and realize I have absolutely no idea what it means to convey.

You mentioned an investigation.

Ongoing, yes. We're constantly on the verge of something, but nothing materializes.

You've got a suspect?

Not in custody, but his identity's no problem.

I only ask, you understand, because of my involvement.

Marge nodded. It's natural.

The problem then is evidence?

Not in so many words. Marge paused, looked up at Knott. I'd tell you more, but you'll laugh.

No I won't.

Yes you will.

No I won't.

Yes you will.

Trust me.

All right. She took a breath. I have a theory.

Knott laughed.

I'm inured, she said. Gray and green—

Bagwell? Sachs?

They think I'm ridiculous too, but the theory is, well, I think the one responsible's somebody else.

You mean like the killer's essentially no one?

In a manner of speaking. The point is, between himself and the shooting there's no connection. I mean, you or I or anybody, if all that didn't have to happen happened as it might've, could just as easily have been, don't you see, him.

So what the murderer knows is—

Personally, I find his reasoning flawless.

—the killer's identity can't be determined.

This morning, Marge said. All the way from my bed to the bathroom, I thought, God's truth, this isn't me, it's my mother!

So you imagine him just standing there, doing what he does, buying cornflakes, fingering the Twinkies, and then out of his pocket comes this gun.

The gun he, of course, knows is in his pocket but never knew was in it, you understand, for something.

And then after the blast, he's as disbelieving as you or me or the old lady back at the refrigerated compartment or, for that matter, the poor slob whose face got blown away.

Marge leaned closer. Can't you just see it? I mean, it's only the whole thing that's unthinkable. Every step's as ordinary as, well, you and me.

Do you ever wonder, Knott asked, if someone represented you, say an actor on tv, so you could, y'know, witness your every move, if maybe you could stand for almost anything?

Marge grabbed her head. Oh I hate that! Questions like that are such a killer!

He looked at her. I want to be frank. I haven't the vaguest idea what my face looks like.

She paused. Like you imagine a blank expression?

I see a peach.

They stared at each other a long moment. Then Marge said: We can't go to my place. It's just been painted.

When Knott arose the next morning he felt unusually certain a night had passed. He strode to the calendar taped on his refrigerator and, with a green crayon, placed a check in the next box in the unbroken succession of checked boxes stretching across his freezer to January. Of course, Knott knew his marks proved nothing. After all, he didn't know if he'd remembered to check a box each previous morning, so that now to commemorate the elapsed night he might actually need to check two or three or, for that matter, any number of boxes. Moreover if, contrary to his waking impression, this were not today but some earlier day starting over again, he might be reliving the earlier day's checking of a box too. In fact, Knott's missing day two days before had produced no break in the succession of his checked boxes, indicating either that checking a box was one of the day's missing events or that the box he was now checking was, in truth, yesterday's, a syncopation in his marking of time that would continue until, through some further chronological idiosyncrasy, his missing day returned.

However, the fact that the woman, of whose body the previous evening Knott still retained such pungent recollections, was no longer in his bed, reinforced Knott's conviction. Now was different from before and in just those ways he customarily told morning from night. At the same time, he found it peculiar that his memory of the woman's departure seemed so lacking. A glimmer of light, perhaps an odor or noise, hardly enough to distinguish from late night tv. Of course, Knott knew himself to be so ignorant, in this and a thousand other cases, of what was and wasn't normal, that her disappearance could well be among the most commonplace of phenomena. All the same, he carefully surveyed the apartment to confirm that the woman's absence was an absence in truth, paying special attention to closets, shower stalls, and curtains where, on the authority of countless old movies, he knew bodies regularly hid. The apartment this morning appeared indistinguishable from the one he'd inhabited the previous evening, all but the door of his medicine cabinet, which while not altered in any particular, nevertheless appeared different in some inexpressible way. Knott examined it full and empty, inventoried his aspirin, ibuprofen, antihistamines, topical anaesthetics, removed the still functioning hinge, tried unsuccessfully to remove the broken, studied its mirror for smudges, fingered, sniffed, and licked it. Everything appeared just as he might've described it had he ever needed—and, in truth, it's not easy to imagine him needing—to describe his medicine cabinet door. Finally Knott hit on the formula, not entirely satisfactory to him but a good deal more so than none, that although he could discern about his medicine cabinet door neither superfluity nor lack, it nevertheless manifested the qualities of a medicine cabinet door from which something recently added had still more recently been taken away. This enabled him to leave for work.

However, at the workplace he discovered further alterations. Someone had turned off his monitor. He checked the desktop, floor, and file cabinets for additional signs of meddling but nothing appeared disturbed. The authorities could still be investigating him, he reflected, or maybe his supervisor was less forgiving than she made out. But then it struck Knott that his intruder could be the one for whom he'd left his questions the previous day. He positioned himself before his computer and lighted the display. There was some whirring, four bars of Jingle Bell Rock, the happy face, then up from the watery depths Knott's screen swam into view:

Knother.

Sure enough, the anonymous writer had been at work, but besides negating Knott's presence, he appeared to have left no trace. Knott tried to make some sense of the elided syllables, but at most they told him what he already knew, that this screen wasn't what he was after, that the solution lay elsewhere, etc. But then the thought struck Knott that the letters might refer to a message concealed in another location. Perhaps Knott's questions were all answered but, instead of appearing automatically on his default screen, the answers were hidden somewhere in his memory. He entered his hard drive, began exploring directories. Almost immediately in a region he rarely visited he found a file labeled LIGHT. It was large and took several seconds to display, but eventually Knott made out the beginning of a story.

The story was about a singer who, through a series of tragic reversals, had lost his voice. None of the singer's misfortunes had damaged his larynx, however. They'd simply given rise to an abiding melancholy which, after several years, turned into a consonance in his head. This sound consisted of neither rising nor falling pitches and did not occur in any time at all. It was merely a single chord that, when heard, had never gone unheard and, when unheard, had never existed. The singer gradually became so absorbed in this chord's abrupt departures and returns that his own voice became unbearable to him. He stopped singing, stopped attending concerts, would seek out the harshest traffic noise to escape any euphony. He eventually withdrew from society altogether, taking up a nocturnal existence of silent attentiveness. Alone he could know perfect, if inconstant, beauty. Among others his anguish was inexpressible.

This plot struck Knott as familiar, although the singer's predicament was inconceivable to him. If it was the murderer's invention, then it merely underscored their differences. However, with the exception of its last episode, Knott could see no connection between the story and the murder. In that episode the singer, driven by want and in periodic despair at his joy's impermanence, went in search of work. Unwilling to venture out except under cover of darkness, he was repeatedly threatened and harassed, and more than one prospective employer mistook him for an assailant. To defend himself, the singer acquired, through an implausible series of chance encounters, a weapon. At first it horrified him. He would circle about it in his room late at night, the inexpressible music resounding in his head. But over time he grew accustomed to its weight and coolness. He practiced discharging it in his imagination, found surprising release in the silent explosions, each unfelt recoil in his shoulder and arm.

The episode broke off abruptly. One morning the singer exited the structure in which he slept, entered a commercial establishment, took his weapon from its hiding place and shot the cashier in the face. No motive was given. It was uncertain whether the murderer knew his victim. In fact, there was a continuous vagueness in the descriptions of the man killed. Several of the sentences recounting the murder were so carelessly written that they failed to distinguish the two individuals, and because the masculine pronoun was used throughout, subject and object were everywhere reversible. Moreover, the shooting was presented from the point-of-view of the victim, an unnamed and otherwise dispensable character who, inexplicably, appeared to know as much about the singer as the narrator did. The author never attempted to justify these inconsistencies. In the terminal sentence, as the weapon exploded, the text described an inexpressible sound pouring out of *his* head for all to hear.

Precisely whose head was meant, however, couldn't be determined.

Knott found this fragment unsettling. At the least, it offered evidence of premeditation, and if its author was indeed the murderer, then it amounted to a virtual confession. However, what Knott found most disturbing was the way it represented its own violence as inevitable. That beauty could cost a man his life seemed uncivilized. For several minutes Knott hesitated over whether to delete the file, hoping by so sweeping a denial to avoid collusion, or to respond to the murder in some more direct way, say, by recounting the singer's arrest or even editing his offense right off the screen. But any action on Knott's part seemed to implicate him more deeply. At last he decided his one recourse was to contact the authorities, relate everything to them, and even if his admissions initially confirmed their doubts, trust in his innocence to absolve him in time. As long as he proceeded with perfect candor, withholding nothing, he could rely on their need for conclusions to bring them around in the end.

Knott had just sent the file to his fax and was beginning to punch in the official number when he heard whispers in the corridor and what sounded like giggling. Opening his door he was startled to find the same suits who had questioned him the day before. Between them stood a round-faced woman and boy about eight.

Remember us? the green asked.

Of course. You're Bagwell, Knott said. Or he is. Anyway, the other one's Sachs.

The green's smile vanished. He's forgotten.

The gray suit shook his head disgustedly. Well it's not like we'd *both* be Sachs, now is it?

Knott drew them into his office. You really couldn't have come at a more perfect time, he said. The killer's been here. I've got evidence!

Suddenly the woman burst into sobs. My Ramon! My Ramon!

The green stepped back. Your chance to talk was yesterday.

Such a good man, a father to his son! she wailed. He worked four jobs!

Knott felt a tugging on his trousers. Mister, why you kill my papa?

What have you been telling these people? Knott demanded.

What'd you think, just because the guy you snuffed was a nobody, the law'd let you forget?

The gray suit leaned closer. We know the whoooooole story.

Side by side with you Ramon he work. How many times his hands give you help? You look my Ramon, your friend, in the eyes, you stab him like a pig in the heart. A devil. I do not see how it is you do this.

I didn't know your Ramon! I never killed anybody's papa!

Oh yeah, that's right, gray said giving a wink. Too busy having a, what was it? Headache.

Un. Con. Scious.

You say to Ramon, we get off the factory we go drinking. But my Ramon he say, no because I am a good man. I go home to my Maria.

It was a convenience store, goddamn it, not a fac—

My papa he buy me the Ken Griffey. He promise to take me to the Marlins. You like the Marlins, mister? They're not so good, but they win a world series—

And so you put the knife in my Ramon because he will not drink the spirits—

No, no, I didn't stab, I shot…I mean your papa, the man who killed him…. Knott turned to the green suit. I don't know what you're up to, but you've got to get these people out of my office. I'll give you a confession. Or a virtual confession.

A man's been murdered, Knott. You got something to say can change that?

The gray sneered. Yeah, who gives a fuck what happened in your head!

This knife it was sooo big. It go in my Ramon and come out behind.

There wasn't any knife!

—blood on the floor, machines. You walk in the blood of my Ramon—

Look, I saw it on the tv. The murderer, he *shot* your Ramon. Or I saw him shoot a cashier.

Tv?

Ramon on tv?

Yes, in a convenience store.

My papa he is an actor?

The gray glared at Knott. Now you've done it!

Is this thing possible?

Well, I mean I saw a security video, Knott said. At the station, they showed me a tv monitor—

But they say you stab Ramon. With long knife. In the heart. Like this. The woman stabbed Knott's chest, neck, etc. They say nothing about the tv. There will be money, no?

Forget the money, the green suit said. There's not gonna be any money.

Is this not the man who killed my Ramon?

Listen lady, your husband's dead. What difference it make if this guy killed him or somebody else?

And this guy, the green pointed at Knott, we got *him* doing it on tv!

My papa he will be on Geraldo?

The gray shook his head at Knott. How could you be so insensitive?

Me!

You are sure it is not Ramon? the woman whimpered.

Knott pointed at the door. If you don't get them out—

Good God, have you no heart?

It is so long time. Maybe if Ramon is actor, he not look like Ramon—

Right now, or I'm calling my supervisor!

The suits exchanged a look. All right, the green finally said, we're going already.

The gray shrugged. No need to get sore.

What Ramon has done with the money?

Out!

The green turned in the door. But next time, try to remember, okay? I'm Bagwell.

Knott spent the rest of the afternoon struggling to recover his composure. What, he kept asking himself, could he be in the midst of? It now seemed clear that his earlier suspicion of a plot had been well-founded. Behind the scenes unknown figures had been contriving his downfall from the start, and if catastrophe weren't to catch him unawares, he'd need to remain conscious of everything. He counseled himself to behave naturally, avoid every act that could lead to inferences, suppress any telling gesture or word. For a long time he sat facing his monitor, the letters on the screen changing from gibberish to mockery to denial:

Knother.

Finally he placed his hands on the keyboard and beneath the letters wrote:

Knott at loose ends. How does his yarn wind up?

He exited his cubicle but, as before, left the machine running.

On the way home Knott was careful to remain conscious of his surroundings, the colors of every shop window, the subtle changes in the trash bins. If his actions were being followed, it would be well to make them as straightforward as possible. The least deviance might be taken for evasion. At the same time he felt unsure that the route he normally traveled was indeed the most direct one. In fact, Knott was pretty certain he'd started walking this way before having any idea where he'd end up, so that now, having come to dwell at his present destination, there was something artificial, even misleading, about just these turns and stops. Maybe, if he'd known what he now knew when he started to work, he might never have traveled this way at all, might have preferred the underground or elevated track or some private means of conveyance. In fact, it almost seemed as if he'd persisted in his path merely because of the countless other figures moving in the same direction. That such an accident could be the explanation of Knott's life struck him as insane. At any rate, his slow progress had gradually become such a matter of indifference to him that the likelihood now of its looking aberrant to others seemed quite alarming. And yet Knott merely had to imagine a perspective with none of the disadvantages of his own to see how this could be the case. Whatever he did literally invited suspicion, and despite his consciousness of all around him, he could figure no new avenue of escape.

By the time he arrived at his home he was frantic. Desperate to elude observation, he rummaged his pockets for the key, but before feeling its rough edge, he noticed his door standing ajar and, coming nearer, heard his shower running. Inside someone's clothes had been strewn over the furniture, the mail was sorted on the end table, and peering into the bathroom, Knott saw his pain medications arranged on the window sill, labels facing out.

Hope you don't mind, Marge called from the shower. The painters seem to be taking forever.

No, no, I-I was hoping to see more of you, Knott began.

How much more do you want? she asked, stepping from the shower.

I mean I would've phoned.

Men! Marge said and slammed the door.

Although Knott found this intimacy with Marge exciting, his walls now seemed less secure than he'd imagined. He tried to calm his heart, slow his breathing. He knew it was probably an overreaction, but she was, after all, connected to the authorities, and even if this gave her access to private places, there still had to be limits. Or had he, in a moment of weakness, given her the key? Either way, he knew he couldn't continue what had begun so promisingly the previous night without getting something straight between them.

We should talk, he said when Marge reappeared.

My idea exactly. She sat down across from Knott, propped her legs up. So, what was your day like?

About us I mean.

Who's us?

I'm being investigated.

If you mean you and the suits—

Gray and green?

—Saxwell and Baggs, I can tell you one thing. Marge gave a long whistle. Boy, are they ticked!

They tried to use a stranger's misfortunes against me.

Oh that. Marge gazed up at the vast unsupported expanse of Knott's ceiling. I was talking about the money.

Money?

When I gave it to them, y'know, I think they felt hoodwinked.

But where'd you get any money?

From the medicine cabinet, Silly. Marge winked at him. Don't worry. I know it isn't yours.

So! Is that what you were doing here last night?

She fell silent. I can't believe you've already forgotten.

Forgotten? I remember exactly!

Then what are you asking me for?

Knott stared at her. Sometimes I think, if I can't explain myself, I'll go mad.

Marge placed her hand on his knee. Let's not get hung up on money, Love. I have news. There's been a breakthrough in your case. I've got a new theory.

Knott laughed.

My theory is, see, the video's just a frame job, the killer's not what you think.

But I saw him!

So you say, but try to see things from our side. Whose word do we have for what you saw but yours? And you, whose word do you have? Maybe what you saw was only a screen.

I don't get it. Why me?

Why me! God, where do you get these questions?

Knott put his face in his hands. You simply have to believe me! The only money I ever had, honestly, was my life savings.

That's asking a lot. Marge sighed. Well, no matter what, Love, promise me, when the suits come around, you won't try the one about working for it.

But it's true! In my cubicle, check the memory, my whole life—

Love, Love, Love, the guy the killer shot, didn't he work too? And where was *his* money? Why, he couldn't even afford a medicine cabinet! So, if working explained it, wouldn't you both have money? But the way the suits will see it, and you know they aren't exceptional, if not everybody working has money, then somebody's getting murdered.

My God, whose side are you on?

How can you ask me that?

Whatever I say, you turn it around like, why, like anybody could've said it!

Marge started to weep. I never dreamed you'd talk to me that way. Haven't I told you my theories, exposed myself to your laughter, concealed nothing, and in return, you treat me like...like your wife.

Knott shook his head. Everything's getting so tangled. I-I just need some time to think.

Think! Anything but that!

Maybe if we spent a night apart...

But what about the paint fumes?

I can call you a hotel.

Go to hell.

The next morning Knott woke up in a fever of remorse. What could have come over him the previous evening? With no Marge he felt bereft, amorphous, pregnable. His earlier suspicions now seemed like a stranger's doing, the delusions of some inane malcontent. Despite her position, Marge had defended his innocence, sought to protect him. Out of what bizarre perversity had he made her the enemy? Knott shook his head. If only he could take back what he'd said. He decided to phone, then realized he'd never asked for her number, a fact that, although he could hardly have not known it, struck him now as new and terrifying. Between himself and all he wasn't stood literally nothing! Struggling to contain his panic, he dressed, forced down some cereal, and fled to work.

Within his cubicle Knott found everything as he'd abandoned it, even his machine running, except that in place of his default screen there was now a message:

> No one can know everything. We both know this, and I know how burdensome knowing it can be. Still, as everybody knows, ignorance is no excuse. A lack of knowledge in the past has only facilitated your work, and you know as well as I that never knowing one's place isn't the same as losing it. Everyone must know something. You know this. I know this. All nobody knows is where, in your case, knowing it will lead. But who knows? Maybe you've made some progress. In any case, let me know.

This summons recalled Knott to a healthy terror of the present. He must retaliate, meet his supervisor's inquiry with the most uncompromising lack of candor. Whenever her reasoning became close, he knew someone would be eliminated, and if Knott was to persist, he'd need to reassure her of his fraudulence and cunning. Suppressing every thought but for survival, Knott marched toward the opening at his corridor's end.

Inside he found his supervisor upon the carpet in what appeared to be profound slumber. However, as soon as Knott stirred she spoke.

Ah Knott, I can't tell you how eagerly, almost like a schoolgirl, I've anticipated your arrival. Why, it's a virtual consummation, don't you think?

Continually. Just to imagine you like this, watching—
But first things first. You've made an advance?

Well, my beginning's misplaced, motivation's still weak, but yes, I'm squarely in the midst of something.

To have come so far without an object, it must be agonizing.

It can be murder.

Personally, I'm filled with admiration, but there are others, you understand, less sublime.

Just yesterday I discovered a plot, any minute I'll have something to hide!

And the pain in your head?

From the time I started taking my medicine—

When you lost consciousness.

Yes, I've felt nothing.

And that, I take it, is good.

It's different. I don't suffer as before.

So, our suspicions weren't groundless? We have reason to fear?

Must something *always* be the matter?

She chuckled. A romantic!

Every turn as wrong as the next, every outcome spoken for, what I really want to say is, well...words fail me.

His supervisor rose to her full height. This world of our making, Knott—famine, madness, waste, disease—it could certainly be without you, and if you're flesh and blood as you maintain, it's likely to continue after you're gone. But if someone were to wonder why you, not not you, not that you're any occasion for wonder, but if, out of restlessness or confusion or some insipid guilt, a body needed reasons, well, surely you don't mean to say, after all these years and my indulgences and the really gruesome outrages necessary to keep it all going, you'd just clam up?

Knott suppressed an urge to grovel. Sometimes when I'm facing my screen, he began, it's like nothing's really wrong. Then this ceaseless din with which I confuse myself, the riot, clatter, it no longer distracts me, and I imagine that, if only through some breach in the conglomerate, word of my silence were to reach you, all the time I'd squandered, my abandoned projects, insistence on having my own loves and pains and terrors as though the countless others before me weren't more than enough, I mean, that all of it might somehow be justified—

Justified! My word!

Or not lacking—

No sooner do I take my eyes off you, Knott, than there you go forgetting yourself.

Really to mean yes, just once, hear, say—

That the accident of you, with your preposterous little intelligence, demanding to be piqued, amused, slaked…that something could justify that!

I-I was speaking figuratively.

Now aren't you ashamed?

What can I say?

Not my problem, Knott, she said dismissing him. But you're almost out of time.

When Knott got back to his cubicle, he forced his trembling fingers onto the keyboard, desperate to compose himself, but the terror that had earlier strengthened his concentration now dispersed it. He stared into one blank screen after another, trying to imagine a change not wholly superfluous, but the prospect of more sentences only depressed him. Who could need them? Maybe the one Knott wasn't but had been while absent had suffered such longings, but with his wits about him now, Knott couldn't help being mindful of everything. Wasn't there some word in the dictionary that simply came next? Finally out of desperation he fled to his default screen, hoping the writer from yesterday had provided inspiration, but all Knott found was nonsense, this time mocking and curtailed:

noher.

If these elisions persisted there'd be no letters left, an outcome that Knott for unclear reasons found disconcerting. Of course, the syllables were a prank, some tasteless word game played at Knott's expense. How did the writer know his

Marge had gone? Or was there some other her Knott was missing? One thing for certain, if the writer found Knott's predicament amusing, then his conclusion would never be the end Knott sought. Knott had never felt so strung out in his life.

He entered the hard drive, started rummaging his memory. If only there were something to build on, no matter how brutal or corrupt. Even a blind assumption would be a start. Almost immediately, in the environs of LIGHT Knott spied a file labeled KNIGHT. For a long moment he stared as though recalling an acquaintance's face. Then something came back. He'd been at an impasse! At what should have been the highpoint of his action, Knott couldn't go on. It was all so vivid and yet vague. The precise obstacle remained in darkness, but Knott felt sure it wasn't anything he didn't know. On the contrary, he recalled that this project differed from others by the clarity with which, from his first presentiments, the whole appeared to him. That was why he'd composed an outline—this file, KNIGHT—so he could find his place if, as had indeed occurred, he forgot where he was.

Knott opened KNIGHT and began to read. He could hardly believe his words! The outline coincided at every point with the writer's story from the day before. Although he found it incredible that longings as immaterial as the unfortunate singer's could've been his creation, he had little choice but to accept it now: the anonymous writer's plot—the inexpressible music and lost voice, solitude, anguish, even the weapon and murder—had all been Knott's invention. LIGHT apparently represented his progress to the point of the impasse. Following the murder, he'd for some reason been unable to go on. But KNIGHT revealed what was to happen next. In Knott's original conception, the singer's isolation was to end. In what stages this was to occur, by what intervening means, or why—all this remained maddeningly inexplicit. But how the unraveling started had been spelled out: at the instant his victim's head burst open, the singer was to recover his voice.

Knott felt like a figure in another's dream. How had he been so sure he wasn't the man in the video? For all he knew the victim's name might have been Ramon! Although it seemed impossible to credit all Marge's misgivings, the absence in his medicine cabinet now appeared telling. That he'd stolen the money was only probable. He'd been in pain. Relief cost. What difference if the crime originated in another's conception or if the murder weapon were discharged by a stranger? Even if facts failed to correspond, Knott's innocence now seemed merely technical. Metaphysically, he was as guilty as anyone. However he imagined it, he knew he must come clean, submit to questions, undergo the worst. He couldn't bear being haunted by what, all things considered, might just as well have been his past as anybody's, and better to be convicted by a jury than by one's own words.

So, let me get this straight, said the suit whose name Knott felt pleased to have remembered was Bagwell. The guy you said you'd never seen before, now you say he's Knott.

That's right. I'm the one behind everything.

So you're confessing—

The guy murdered on tv, he died because of me.

But why the convenience store? the other suit, necessarily Sachs, put in. I mean, was it personal, a grudge, some woman?

I remember being in pain. Maybe I needed an aspirin.

You said there was a doctor, Bagwell added helpfully.

Yes, he wrote it all down.

His name, you can imagine, would be a big help.

It was dirty. Not the name exactly, but y'know, like it.

Grimes?

Ashe?

Rank?

Mudd?

Mudd's dirty all right, but y'know, not really his name.

So, if he wrote you a prescription, wouldn't a drug store be more logical?

First a dentist, now a doctor. What'll he complain of next?

Bagwell smiled. We appreciate your being so guilty, Knott, but your story's still got to hold up.

Knott sat facing a wall identical to the wall he'd faced when questioned before, only this wall, quite possibly the same one, had recently been painted purple. The fumes were asphyxiating.

There's so much to explain, Knott sighed. Couldn't I just watch the video?

Here we go again! Sachs rolled his eyes.

Who's we? Knott asked.

Are, Sachs corrected.

Maybe I could get you something to drink? Bagwell offered getting up.

Do you have Perrier? Knott turned to Sachs. Who's R?

Bagwell chuckled. He means we's plural, like you.

We's plural?

With a twist? Bagwell asked.

You's plural; me's singular, Sachs explained irritably. We may seem peculiar, since it's first person, like I, so perhaps it feels like there should only be one, but I assure you, we's every bit as plural as you is.

Lime if you have it, Knott answered. He observed that Bagwell had switched to a blue suit today, while Sachs was wearing a brown. Although these new colors combined disagreeably with the purple wall, their change created no problem of identity. Knott simply recalled the colors from the day before and aligned them according to the scheme: green/blue, gray/brown. Of course, he knew that yesterday he might have already confused identities, in which case Bagwell could still be Sachs, even if blue today.

But to return to your question, Bagwell said, we represent our state.

Us of America, Sachs put in.

Plural.

Or a collective really, Sachs qualified. Like the majority or queen—

In the bottle, Bagwell asked, or over ice?

—and in that socio-political sense, you see, Sachs concluded, you and he and I, although in other respects opposed, may be considered all one.

Which question? Knott asked

With a twist or in the bottle? Sachs offered.

Who's we? Bagwell put in.

Are, Sachs corrected.

But *who's* R? Knott demanded.

Whose are? Are you mad? Sachs roared. Why everybody's! I mean if you speak English!

His point, Bagwell put in, is simply that when you ask us for our identities, the proper form of be is are. He gave a worried glance in Sachs' direction.

B is R?

Not really, or no more bizarre than having no future for must or no past for may or—

ARE IS NOT A NAME! Sachs shrieked.

Bagwell's smile was conciliatory. Wait now, seems like I remember. Wasn't he the guy who wrote that awful book? About Michelangelo.

R?

You're confusing him with the author.

They had the same name—

Does no one want to hear my confession? Knott asked.

Sachs looked at Bagwell.

Bagwell looked at Knott.

Knott looked at Sachs.

These fumes are nauseating, Sachs said standing up. I'll go for the Perrier.

Bagwell sat down. Okay, tell us about the weapon.

Don't you mean the money?

Bagwell colored. We know about the money, thank you.

Marge says it—

We *know*!

Knott stared at the wall. It struck him that, by contrast, the purple made Bagwell's red face seem quite pale, which might have been the rationale for the color. On the other hand, there might be no rationale for the color, which might also be a rationale, since you couldn't help wondering, why purple?

F'rinstance, where'd you get the pistol?

What's the difference? A gun's a gun isn't it?

Christ, a person would think you didn't watch prime time. Here's the routine. First, we make you tell your story, then we trick you into turning over the murder weapon, then we're gonna need a body—

Knott jumped up. You mean you don't have a body?

Suddenly the door swung open and, to Knott's amazement, Marge walked in. She was carrying a green bottle, wedge of lemon and a glass of ice. Somebody wanted this? she asked.

Knott smiled. Yes, yes, I can't tell you how—

She turned to Bagwell. You getting anywhere with the dipstick?

We're doing perfectly well, thank you, Bagwell responded icily.

I just thought I could—

Thank you, Bagwell interrupted. Was there anything else?

Knott spoke. Personally, I'd like for Marge—

Both the woman and Bagwell whirled on him. Who asked *you*?

I just meant, knowing Marge as I do, I'd be more comfortable—

Comfortable! the woman guffawed.

Who's Marge? Bagwell asked.

Anyway, the old bat's ready if you are, she said.

About the paint fumes, Knott began.

Marge looked at Bagwell.

Bagwell looked at Marge.

They burst out laughing.

Can you believe this guy? Bagwell said chortling.

Priceless, Marge said. She stepped into the corridor. Bring 'er in!

An elderly woman entered leaning on a cane and followed by a wilting Sachs.

—out of my own living room, the very idea, savage, and on a Thursday which ask anybody is the day we play canasta, anybody, always has been, since before—

We feel really bad about the inconvenience, ma'am, but if you'd just—

This the one? the old woman snapped, glaring at Knott. Something about the curve of her spine seemed familiar.

That's, you understand, what we hoped you'd tell—

She silenced him with a flip of her hand. You may think just because I'm old I don't know what's what, but believe you me, I watch television. She wobbled toward the table, fixing Knott every step with her eyes. For a long moment she inspected him, then turned to Bagwell. Can it stand?

Get up, Bagwell said.

Knott stood. Now I remember, he said. You were in the video, at the refrigerated compart—

You shut up, Bagwell said.

Yeah, none of this concerns you, Sachs put in.

The lady tottered over to Knott's shoulder, looked him up, down, inspected his shoes, then gave a nod and started out. Not him.

Are you sure? Sachs asked opening the door.

Too short, she said.

But it was all so fast—

I know what I know!

What about his face?

Didn't see his face.

So how can you—

I told you! I know what I know!

Sachs shrugged, closed the door.

Bagwell turned to Knott. Listen, I'm not going to lie to you. Things aren't looking good. Unless you can come up with something new, well, you're gonna walk outa here.

Knott pulled a computer disk from his pocket. Here, he said. I know it all seems cloudy, but this'll make everything black and white.

Bagwell held the disk up to his face. KNIGHT LIGHT, he said. He handed it back. So?

No, I mean, put it in your machine.

Do I look like some geek to you?

Well, surely you've got someone here who can use a computer!

Bagwell shook his head. Boy, you just don't get it, do you? Here's the routine. I show you a video, you say it's not you, then later you say it is you. You show me a disk, you say it is you, then maybe later you say it's not you. He leaned closer. We aren't after another *version*.

You want me to kill somebody right in front of you?

If that's the best you can do.

But I'll make a full confession!

No motive, no weapon, no body. You can't expect us to just take your word.

There was a loud knock. Sachs appeared at the door. Found him, he said. Everything checks out.

Bagwell turned to Knott, sighed. Sorry pal, looks like you're innocent.

Found who? Knott asked.

Dr. Mudd, Bagwell said.

Clay, Sachs corrected.

Whatever, Bagwell said. The dentist.

Endodontist really, Sachs said.

And I was right? Knott asked. He remembered me.

The toothache, Sachs explained, he remembered the toothache. After you got gassed, he says you were out of your mind.

So I haven't been faking?

Bagwell sighed. If the doctor says you hurt, then you hurt.

But there's got to be more to it than that.

Nope, evidently you were somewheres else.

But I'm capable of murder, don't you think? I mean, it can't be out of the question. I imagined everything!

Killer wasn't you. End of story.

But that's just an accident of timing.

Makes all the difference in the world.

You've got to look at this! Knott thrust the computer disk under Sachs' nose. It *had* to happen.

Tell it to somebody who cares, Sachs said walking out.

Magenta, Knott thought as the door closed. Not purple, magenta.

All that night Knott was assailed by nightmares of vanishing horizons, and next morning he awoke in a comatose funk. Instead of relief at being absolved, he felt depleted, as though someone had plundered his private safe. All that had formerly made such a difference to him, his blindness and lies, the imaginable transgressions, all now seemed, not decimated exactly, but dispelled, reduced to hand wringing. Could every atrocity he'd ever committed really have been committed by just anyone? No matter how painful facing up had proven before now, Knott had always felt prepared, but how to face up to having nothing to face up to?

He dressed, headed for the workplace, hoping at each step to be accosted by the families of unknown victims, lives he'd eliminated unawares, but none of the eyes on the street looked in his direction. His workplace too appeared without distinction. His chair felt as though it had never supported him, and his desk, stapler, pencils, paper clips, seemed ready for absolutely anything. Phone silent, screen blank.

Determined to locate his misdeeds, Knott began searching his hard drive for LIGHT then KNIGHT, but all he could find were tiny numbers and symbols. Evidently, while he'd been unconscious the night before, a power surge had jumbled his memory, or possibly the network's wires had gotten crossed. Whatever, Knott's crimes were now a thing of the past. He considered calling the number Bagwell had given him—perhaps there'd been new developments, some fresh grounds for suspicion—but when he pulled the slip of paper from his wallet, it turned out to be a dry cleaning receipt, and the illegible name scrawled on the back began with an R. It seemed that he had no choice but simply to write down whatever occurred to him, which this morning felt like conceding failure from the start. He stared at his screen, wondering where the missing letters could possibly come from, then without considering what he was doing, he typed at the top:

But this was not the end!

Knott paused. What followed the recovery of voice? For a long time he gazed into the blankness before him, waiting, perfectly still. Somewhere in the walls of the building an engine began to hum. He heard footsteps passing in the corridor. A door opened, closed. Then his keyboard began to click, slowly at first, then resuming, a short burst, increasing steadily until the soft rattle became a stampede. It took him all morning and much on his display remained fragmentary, but by lunchtime Knott's denouement was complete.

The end began with the singer's return to the stage. Although years passed before concert-masters would accept his recovery and audiences forgive him, in time the mature singer achieved the success his youthful misfortunes had delayed. Some felt his voice had actually improved during its retirement, and although a few still missed the unspoiled tenor, most felt the baritone's darkness more than compensated any loss.

But the singer was not at peace. Privately he was haunted by his faceless victim. Having recognized the dead man's spirit in the audience one evening, he'd sought the specter out, and in no time the two had become companions. As the singer's renown grew, the lifeless being occupied more and more of his consciousness. The singer would wake in the dark to find his shattered skull peering down at him, or he'd return from rehearsal to meet the blasted visage waiting before his fire. Although the gunshot had deprived the spirit of his tongue, he remained unusually animated for a dead man, and by means of gestures, he and the singer managed to communicate. However, his facelessness was a barrier to intimacy with others. This disturbed the singer. In life, he learned, the dead man had been convivial, and the thought that his music, which was the singer's sole expression, had made of his companion a blank, seemed too painful to endure. How could something so beautiful have been so devastating? What sort of being, the singer wondered, had his voice put an end to?

His performances began to suffer. His attack, universally praised for its authority, now gave way to hesitation. At times his portrayals bordered on self-parody, and one critic accused him of coloring phrases to hedge articulation. Although the singer continually exhorted himself, correcting every slip, his success now showed signs of effort. What had become of his youthful inspiration, his admirers asked, that inexpressible consonance which had formerly taken the world away?

One evening the singer could bear the applause no longer. Overcome with self-loathing, he rushed back to his dressing room to beg the spirit's help. He simply had to know what facelessness felt like! Did the dead man still weep, only unbeknownst to others? Or was his expressionlessness so utter he could now countenance everything? The poor spirit was unable to respond at first and merely withdrew into his gloom, but finally he intimated there might be hope. In a flurry of gestures he explained that, although blankness was of all suffering the hardest to enter into, if the singer's remorse was genuine, then he had only to yield his voice to the being he'd defaced to penetrate its depth. The singer was taken aback. A surrender so complete would mean his undoing! Under the spirit's power, who knew what pandemonium he'd give in to? But he realized he could face the music no other way. And so, after much agonizing, the singer acquiesced.

The end came rapidly. He continued for a brief time to perform, but his voice now seemed a ghost of its former self. At each rest in the music outlandish departures struggled for release, and with every fresh attack his singing underwent spasms of tone and pitch. Listeners grew confused, their approval tentative. All but the most loyal drifted off, and then one night in an orgy of pent-up frustration, his admirers leaped to their feet and, halfway through a monstrous aria, started to boo and bang their seats. It was a riot. The orchestra fled, costumes were ripped off. The singer barely escaped with his life.

Not since his youth had he felt so abandoned. Even his companionable victim appeared to have deserted him. But there was something else too. The noises escaping him now certainly weren't music, or no music he'd ever known, but neither were they unheard of. Instead, they seemed to recall music's outcast soul or daemon, a being neither pleasing nor harsh but utterly arresting, as though the end he'd always been listening for were now constantly under way.

Knott knew there had to be more. Staring into his computer, he felt the singer's fate unravel past the screen's edge. But now that he'd achieved the singer's undoing, Knott couldn't for the life of him remember why he'd cared to. He made a ludicrous attempt at a concluding tableau—the singer standing in a meadow surrounded by goats and cowbirds as an indescribable cacophony filled the air—then got up from his desk. He felt famished. Knott exited his cubicle to look for something to eat.

Once outside Knott prowled the nearby cafes and sandwich shops like an escaped animal, but his body's craving would fix on nothing. Finally on a street identical to the streets he traversed every day, at an identical table in an identical cafe, he spied a woman identical to the woman he'd known two days earlier as Marge. Knott hesitated, recalling their recent misadventure and Marge's coolness at his interrogation. Still, if she was she and he could only manage to be himself, why couldn't everything continue as before? Knott approached the woman's table, then when her head failed to come up from her book, gave a timid cough.

I thought I'd seen the last of you, he offered.

Excuse me?

No need, really. He sat down. In fact, that was what I wanted to say. I mean, about all that happened. For me it's just like we'd never met.

The woman continued to regard Knott with an astonishment he found far from encouraging. There seems to be a misunderstanding, she said at last. You are laboring under illusions that, I hasten to assure you, are none of my doing. However, to avoid needless pain, I release you from all imaginary obligations. Feel free to go.

But I was hoping I could make it up to you?

It?

You see, back in the dark while we were lying together, I kept imagining another person. It's an old story I know, but, well, I'm finished with it now.

He noticed Marge had picked up her fork and was gripping it in her fist. Sir, she said, unless you leave this table at once, I'll be forced to take measures we'll both regret. Is there no place on earth you'd rather be?

Knott stared at her. He'd never known his Marge to be so unyielding. The longer he studied her face, the less familiar it looked. Could this really *be* someone else? Or had he fallen in love with a perfect stranger?

Weren't you Marge? he finally asked.

Looks I've heard—or is it books? Anyway, covers can be deceiving.

Incredible!

Take my word, nothing remotely like it has ever occurred to me.

Knott shook his head. And yet the way we're talking together, so naturally—

All at once the woman dropped her face into her hands and began to sob. I remember *nothing*! *Nothing*! she cried. Maybe she was me. How should I know? They expect me to act so preposterously, all these costumes, the tattoos, hair coloring. To be perfectly frank it's been years since I knew whose life I was living. It's my position, you see. I don't expect you to understand.

They?

And as for this body you enjoyed, couldn't it have been mine as much as anyone's? I mean in the dark, how much difference is there really? You needn't answer. I'm unspeakably pleased to learn bliss was yours—what could be better? But all the same, even if I was her, this is something else. I'm Merideth by the way.

So there's no Marge?

People change. My friends call me Merry.

Knott stared at the face staring into his face. Minutes earlier he'd felt the greatest urgency to revive in this woman's countenance what, now that he'd begun to reflect on it, seemed impossible to picture there. Exactly what object he'd formerly had in view he couldn't begin to say. Even his appetite, though by no stretch of the imagination satisfied, was gone. He stood up.

I apologize. Apparently I mistook you for someone different.

But I *am* someone different!

A woman beside yourself, I mean. It was just a theory.

Merideth laughed.

Strange, he said, how vivid it all was.

What you were saying you mean?

Hardly. He held out his hand. Forgive me.

Merideth stared at it. And that's just it?

What more would you have?

You come between me and my reading, tell me your theories, question everything, and now you expect me to act like nothing ever happened?

Knott stared at her a moment longer. Not exactly, he said.

When Knott got back, his workplace appeared transfigured. There'd been no alteration to the structure, but he had the strongest impression he'd entered by a different door. Light shone from every surface, unfamiliar voices echoed in the rooms, the corridors extended forever. At a turn he bumped into his supervisor, and although she smiled, he noticed she was listing badly and seemed to confuse him with someone named Ramon. There were no labels on the doors, no exit signs or windows. Knott had to go to unusual lengths to find his opening.

At last he arrived at a cubical indistinguishable from the cubicle in which he'd wound up his yarn. He felt literally exhausted, but nothing essential appeared missing. He turned on the machine, heard distant whirring, eight bars of Rocky Mountain High, waited for the happy face, then his default screen swam into view.

Light destorys darkness.

He stared at the sentence a long time. That it had occurred to him by accident seemed of no account now. The words were his as much as anyone's. Possibly more. All that remained was to pick up the last thread, carry his sentence out. Knott waited. In a moment a soft knock could be heard at the door.

You've got the key, he called out.

The door opened. In the corridor stood the murderer from the convenience store. He wore a brown jacket of the same style as Knott's brown jacket and had thinning hair identical to his. Although his expression was utterly blank, Knott was struck by what seemed his pathetic lack of reserve. In one hand he held an aspirin bottle.

You're Knott, are you not? the murderer sighed.

I've been dying to know myself, Knott replied almost gaily.

I figured as much. And now?

Knott made a sweeping gesture. See? I'm in a new place.

You mean you're closer?

Well, distance was never the headache.

No? The murderer lowered himself into a chair, fixed Knott with his stare. Then what'd you want me for?

Knott smiled. No telling.

Well, thank God that's over.

history

Preface

All will agree that the publication of this volume is a bold undertaking. Some may think it arrogant. The editors are not insensitive to this charge. To speak on behalf of another is always risky business, and the risks are increased when that other can no longer respond. Such risks are familiar to scholarship. But to speak in the name of another, to appropriate to oneself the life of his or, as in this case, her mind, to assume an authority not one's own...this goes beyond mere risk. It appears to be presumption. It may be fraud.

When on an August afternoon three years ago Dr. Myra Q. Stitz gazed up into the blue windshield of a careening parcel delivery van and concluded upon the asphalt of Meridian's commercial boulevard forty-three years of inspired and vigorous teaching, we, her colleagues and students, feared our own lives had come to an end. We'd sat across from her at tables, beside her in bars, walked with her at night among the grain bins and along the canal and always something was growing. When we spoke well, she'd jab her cigar at us: "Yes! Yes!" When we stumbled, she'd wait. We insisted that she publish her reflections, but she always laughed. "Whose reflections do you mean?"

In her two-room apartment above a musical instrument repair shop in this small southeastern town, Dr. Stitz left behind her, among the peculiar detritus of her personal life, a mass of writing too chaotic, fragmentary and tentative to constitute an opus but too daringly original to be ignored. For eleven months Dr. Peter Schleeter-Nachter studied these loose sheets, crumpled notes, and annotated journals trying to determine what existed in a state appropriate for publication. He read esoterica, phantasmal calculations, playful "hypothesisettes"—as Dr. Stitz liked to call them— all manner of abstruse speculation perhaps never intended to be read at all. There was a wholeness present, he informed us, a tone, a style of mind. Recognition seemed always about to take shape, but the Myra we'd known had vanished among the parts.

As Dr. Stitz's executors we were faced with clear alternatives. First, we might publish nothing under the name of Dr. Stitz herself. Her papers could be entered in the manuscript collection of the college library, and when utilizing her work in our own writing we could acknowledge the source and our indebtedness. Aside from an aura of professional opportunism surrounding this course of action, we disliked it for other reasons as well. Dr. Stitz's work deserved more attention than the preservation of her papers in a college library could insure. We knew that the writings of several individuals, no matter how directly influenced by that of Dr. Stitz, could never adequately represent the original. We decided against this alternative.

Second, we might publish her work precisely as we found it. This would raise a variety of practical difficulties involving the presentation of multiple versions, apparent revisions, strike-throughs, frivolous insertions, self-parodies, variant schemes of organization, manuscript illegibilities, discontinuities, and transliteration of her (often exotic) idiolect, but these might be overcome with the assistance of an imaginative printer and a minimal amount of editorial discretion.

Our objection to this course was theoretical. We believed that Dr. Stitz's thought was much more coherent than such a presentation would demonstrate. Anyone who had ever sipped tea with her (Dr. Stitz drank no coffee or whiskey and refused to think whenever these were served; however, she had an inordinate love of Assam tea, trifle, hard cider, stout and, most notoriously, an unnamed but hideously noxious brand of Cuban cigar) knew well Dr. Stitz's methodological self-consciousness and consistency of intention. Her arguments were fragmentary but not without strongly implied hierarchies, parallelisms, and a distinctive syntax. We concluded that the larger context of her café dialogues, peripatetic meditations, lectures, and informal chats were demanded by her writing. We emphatically rejected this second alternative.

Third, we might write her work. This is, of course, what we have done. Wherever possible we have used Dr. Stitz's own words, examples, non-standard orthography and punctuation. Where her notes were fragmentary or wherever her argument existed in outline only, we have paraphrased, interpolated and assembled her meaning. We have not always agreed among ourselves, as evidenced by the alternative renderings in chapters three and eight (points where Dr. Stitz apparently did not agree with herself!). Much has been omitted. In the appendix we have included facsimiles and transcripts of some relevant materials.

Can such a method be justified? We are uncertain. Are we attempting to give to a secondary work the authority of a primary one? Surely there is interpretation here, but whose? Nothing is concealed from the reader except what remains concealed from us all.

We make no apologies. If editorial responsibilities have ever been assumed honestly (and despite frequent abuses, we believe there *is* honesty in editorship), then we maintain that ours is an instance of such honesty. More importantly, if our undertaking can be justified, then the work of Dr. Myra Stitz will provide that justification. "We think me," she says in her first sentence, and then follows the fanciful "Parable of the Lonely Termite Who was Not." For Dr.

Stitz, consciousness is so radically social that she could maintain (as she often did with her tea sloshing dangerously in her upraised cup and her cigar pounding on the table edge like a gavel) that "nine thinkers are required for one clear idea and a whole suburb for an insight." Minds are a property of conversations. No one author's thinking. To anyone objecting that such reflections are mere editorial self-justification, we can only echo Dr. Stitz's own words: "Whose reflections do you mean?" We believe *Refractions of Identity* by Myra Q. Stitz offers an answer. We welcome all sincere critical response.

P. S-N.
S. S. S.
Meridian College

Preface to the Revised Edition

Myra Stitz lives.

When the first of R. F. Drew's memoirs, "Dialogue at The Blue Potato," appeared in *Eidos* three years ago, all admirers of Myra Stitz were startled, none more so than her editors. Many of you will have followed the lengthy debate and ensuing correspondence in *Codices* between Mr. Drew and two of us—Drs. Peter Schleeter-Nachter and Stephen Sneed. Some may have examined the facsimile edition of Dr. Stitz's "manuscripts"—her assorted cocktail napkins, claim checks, envelope flaps, journal margins and flattened tissue boxes—published last summer by Epigone Press. All who knew Dr. Stitz will remember her hearty faith in the exuberance of mind: "Discourse is more fertile than we are. It cannot be aborted." A decade after her death her editors finally understand what she means.

Myra Q. Stitz did not write *Refractions of Identity*. In their attempt to construct an authoritative text, the editors of the first edition suppressed Dr. Stitz's most daring insights, abandoned the tone and arrangement these implied, and substituted much inferior material of their own. These inadequacies became apparent with the publication of the now infamous "Third Conversation at The Blue Potato" (a vegetarian eatery frequented by Dr. Stitz and recently taken over by the Meridian College Credit Union). Mr. Drew and Dr. Stitz had been engaged in a lengthy and, for Drew, frustrating discussion of baseball and coercion. Drew reports:

> I kept trying to paraphrase her remarks in terms of the sociology of knowledge (I'd been listening to John Cage) and looked for her approval. She only sucked her cigar and snorted. Finally I blurted out that she must consider me "dense." She eyed me for a moment, then reached over and pressed her thumb against my forehead. "Precisely, Drew. Nothing passes through you." Afterwards she got very drunk and kept muttering something about "social boundaries," but I was too discomposed to make it out.

Here was a new Myra Stitz! We could speculate endlessly about the lost "boundaries" utterance, but one thing was certain: this Dr. Stitz was fascinated by solidity. "Whatever we cannot penetrate we must try to understand," she remarks in the previously unpublished twenty-second conversation (included in the appendix to this volume). A host of forgotten observations returned to the memories of her editors. We now realized that her first sentence, "We think me," referred to something far more fundamental than society, and immediately her entire volume began to rethink itself.

The new edition was begun. Nightly we gathered in the Meridian College Library to sift scraps of paper and argue. Spirits were high. Often we failed to hear the closing buzzer and had to grope for the exits in the dark. Whenever one of us made a discovery we'd all shout. The librarians considered us a nuisance. Despite our former intimacy with Dr. Stitz, we felt as if we had never known her until now. In the words of our senior member, "I catch myself asking her questions. It's like walking along the canal again. At times I'm sure I smell the cigars."

As Mr. Drew's *Memoir* suggested and our subsequent research revealed, much more of Dr. Stitz's work remained unwritten at her death than we'd first believed. Again and again we'd mistaken pauses for closure, and now the intricacy of her plan seemed startling. Chapters two and five became "Meditation Twelve: Whereabouts," the "utility fragments" were relegated to the appendix, and the Algebra of Ground $(f(U)=M_e^2)$ had to be dispersed throughout. Still greater boldness was required for this edition than formerly, and yet our sense of direction was much surer. Dr. Stitz was beginning to speak to us through her silences. Incompleteness, we realized, had always been her intention. As she explains in the fifty-third conversation, "Only dead things are whole."

And now we are approaching an answer to the questions we first raised nearly a decade ago. Myra Stitz's editors have not written her work, as we formerly believed. Her work has written, and continues to rewrite, itself. "Who thinks for the jazz quartet?" she muses in a characteristic comparison. "The saxophone switches to swing, the brushes start to skip and slide, the piano player's hands catch the rhythm before he does. Afterwards the bass man remarks, 'We were just playing and the changes were there.'" What had before seemed editorial hubris now revealed itself as dull-witted resistance to the force of Myra Stitz's mind. We offer here no commentary, no extrapolation, and certainly no original work. *Refractions of Identity* has come into its own. The editors were there.

S. S. S.
P. S-N.
R. F. D.
Meridian College

Preface to the Critical Edition

The publication of this edition of *Refractions of Identity* is principally remarkable for its occurrence. As few as six years ago, no one would have believed it possible. Skepticism remains rampant. The editors are themselves by no means immune. The purpose of this preface is to deal as forthrightly as possible with the problems of the Myra Q. Stitz legacy in hope of, if not resolving all doubt, then at least distancing the present edition from those that have preceded it.

Before the revised edition was ever dust-jacketed, one of us, Dr. Derwent Irwin of the Hoagland Institute, had already made the discovery that would utterly discredit it. Had the printing been delayed six months it would not have occurred. As Dr. Irwin first revealed in his disturbing editorial, "Fraud!" (*Parles-tu?*, vol. XV, no. iiii), R. F. Drew enrolled in Dr. Stitz's survey "Problems of Impure Mathematics" during the fall of 1964 but withdrew for undetermined reasons at the end of the first week. He continued to attend lectures at Meridian College until November of that year when he emigrated to Canada in order to evade the draft and a possible narcotics conviction. Although there is some evidence to support his claim of a personal acquaintance with Dr. Stitz, it is clear such an acquaintance was much too brief to have included even a minute portion of the over one hundred "conversations" contained in his *Memoir*. When confronted with these charges it is to Mr. Drew's credit that he denied nothing and offered as his only defense the substantial plausibility of his inventions. "Even if it never happened," he maintained in a privately circulated statement *Eidos* refused to print, "it might have." A clever argument but in present context a straightforward admission of deceit.

The reaction of Dr. Stitz's other editors was considerably less straightforward. Drs. Stephen Sneed and Peter Schleeter-Nachter refused to acknowledge they had authored over three hundred of the text's seven hundred fifty-three pages, despite Alban B. Cuda's damning stylistic analysis, "A Work of Many Hands" (*Parles-tu?*, vol. XV, no. iiiiiii). Arguing from such Stitzian conceptions as antidefinition and the immortality of data, Sneed and Schleeter-Nachter maintained the fundamental passivity of their roles. When questioned in *Codices* regarding plagiarism, documentation and authority, they appeared alarmingly insensitive to the ethical issues involved. "The author's work is whatever fits," Dr. Sneed asserted in his only editorial defense, and Dr. Schleeter-Nachter seemed willing to extend himself still farther: "Why is everyone so stirred up about handwriting? So what if it is *my* handwriting? Would anyone doubt it's *her* idea?" In a letter of only nine paragraphs, Dr. Sneed appealed twelve times to the "spirit" of Dr. Stitz's work. Such loose thinking obscures essential distinctions to a degree that is criminal.

The work of Myra Q. Stitz must be dissociated from this sophistry and moral obtuseness. Although we cannot easily dismiss the editorial dilemmas raised by the previous editions or the theoretical enigma of authorship itself, we can eschew all subterfuge. In preparation for this volume the editors returned to the three "alternatives" (sic) of the original preface. The first "alternative" not to publish anything at all became for us the question whether a new *Refractions* could be justified, a question easily answered by the vast quantity of provocative writing generated over the last two decades by Dr. Stitz's followers. Despite professional risks and an intimidating climate of public hostility, we concluded that Dr. Stitz had proven too influential to be left in adulterate and piecemeal form.

The second "alternative," to publish the Stitz manuscripts precisely as they existed in the Meridian College Library, was both simpler and far more complicated for us than for the original editors. Simpler because the Epigone Press facsimile had done just this. Of course, there are lingering questions here (the "backward slanting fragments" discussed by Prof. Cuda ["Stitz's Many Scripts," *Parles-tu?*, vol. XV, no. iiiiiiiiiiiiiii] and the two tissue flaps carbon-testing has dated three years after Dr. Stitz's death), but the facsimile does provide a basically reliable text for those to whom (in Dr. Schleeter-Nachter's disparaging phrase) "graphology is the principal test of authorship."

The complication arose from our inability to repudiate the most problematic assertions of the original editors. There does seem to be a coherence to the Stitz fragments, and this coherence seems most intelligible when viewed against the background of Dr. Stitz's personal conversations, musings, and "spoken works." Although we sought to qualify this bold claim with objective evidence—student lecture notes, Dr. Stitz's unpublished doctoral dissertation, a paper delivered at a Hunter college colloquium twenty years prior to her death—no document could entirely refute it. Dr. Stitz's thinking deserved publication in its most attractive form. Any arrangement, even that of the facsimile, required a certain amount of speculation, a certain amount of editorial daring.

Which returned us to the notorious "third alternative." But here we had to pause. We refused to "write her work" for her as the original editors had claimed to do. As the textual history has shown, any crossing of the boundaries between author and editor opens the way for abuses without limit. What we have decided upon is the present variorum. The sequence is roughly that of the revised edition (regarding this sequence see Prof. Cuda's essay "Graphemic Diachronicity, Non-linear Structuring, Spectroscopic Ink Analysis, and the Case for Sequence in the Manuscripts of Myra Q. Stitz," *Parles-tu?*, vol. XV, no. iiiiiiiiiiiiiiiiiiiiiiiiiiiiiiiiiii) with cross references to the original edition (Arabic numerals in brackets) and the Epigone Press facsimile (Roman numerals in parentheses). Only in doubtful cases have we begun a section with a typographic reproduction of an entire fragment, although at points of unusual difficulty we have included cross references and possible sources, variants, and early drafts. All editorial interpolations, paraphrasing, footnotes, punctuative and orthographic standardization, splicing, insertions, "corrections," and occult exemplification have been set off in bold face. After introductory remarks concerning the rationale of former editors, we have placed the edited versions themselves along with our critiques of them, followed by a(n admittedly speculative) reconstruction of the composition history of those fragments upon which the section is (probably) based and excerpts from pertinent (?) conversations, recollected remarks, and student notes culminating in our attempt at a tentative, restrained textual reconstruction with appended documents, article reprints, and in three cases, extracts from particularly "plausible" sections of Mr. Drew's *Memoir* with explanatory notes and addenda. We regret the twelve volume format. Some will complain there has been a great sacrifice of "readability"; we fear this is so. There is about the whole project an air slightly pedantic, and this is all the more painful because of our boyish enthusiasm for it. We can only say in defense that, at last, the distinction between editor and author is clear, and we hope textual reliability with its soberer satisfactions will compensate readers for the loss of more ephemeral pleasures. Any student can now distinguish what is Dr. Stitz herself, what is editorial intrusion, what is (imperfect) recollection, what is plausible reconstruction, what is synthesis and paraphrase, what is well-intended speculation, what is fraud. The amassed whole of *Refractions of Identity*, which has obscured so much falsification and distortion, is finally undone. All lovers of Myra Q. Stitz can examine the parts for themselves.

D. U. I.
A. B. C.
et al.
Hunter College

Preface to the New Stitz

Perhaps the fraud is not so much that of author or editor but of identity itself. Perhaps the lie is the conviction from the start that we are not each other. Then plausibility is as much as can be asked, the fullest, and composition becomes the task of making whole. It is a shared responsibility. Even analysis has a place, but the end of all labor is binding together. One tries very hard to be amusing.

We are Myra Q. Stitz and have written nothing until now. Drew, Irwin, Sneed are ciphers—edition's multiplication. The variorum, being accurate, may be ignored. The question arises: can Stitz become her desire? This is not the first time they've pronounced us dead.

We shall now reveal several anecdotes our editors never knew. Once upon a time while teaching at Meridian College we fell in love with water and forgot how to speak. Our students already understood that every new idea was a vessel. "Board her," we often advised, "or sink." Then one afternoon a young woman with no eyebrows and a carbuncle on her cheek—we can still see her—confessed with a yawn that all this talk of oceans "bored her." The faces in the room turned deathly pale. With a decorous sweep of our arm we dismissed class and stood gazing out the window for two days. How was anything intelligible? Many years after our untimely death this question continues to disturb those who vainly seek us in our writings.

Last spring we walked once again on the banks of the old canal and discussed this problem with our intimate friends, R. F. Drew and Alban Cuda. They referred frequently to Linwood Amory's recent discussion of continuity ("More! More! More!" *Odium*, 6/9), and because of our long association with these men, their enthusiasm became our own. We invited Dr. Amory to meet with us in the Meridian College Library, and soon amid the heady fume of Cuban tobacco we were all ourself again. The long experience of emeritus professors Sneed and Schleeter-Nachter provided reassurance, and Derwent Irwin's intellectual integrity forced us beyond old solutions. "*Refractions of Identity* is NOT Myra Stitz!" he often reminded us. Or something like that.

We were convinced. With Mr. Drew's guidance we recalled the period in our life of the Deep Silence. "She began to drink stout for breakfast, belch in committee, ingest her cigars," he told us. "If you greeted her in the corridor, her lips would flap wordlessly, her face turn away." Dr. Sneed recollected how he encouraged us to confide our anguish. "I felt so helpless. All afternoon you'd hear her bedroom slippers scraping over the linoleum in her office. The secretaries complained she was monopolizing the staff toilet, standing before the sink, both spigots twisted open, gazing for hours into the mirror as the spew of hot and cold swilled down the drain." Until now this period has been disregarded for fear of raising doubts about the finality of our conclusions, but no longer. As Prof. Cuda (who was our student at this time) was first to understand, we were preparing for our loftiest insight. "Dr. Stitz spent each class session cleansing herself of all her old conceptions. She would sweep into the room in a white gown, her hair patchy, nested, her slippers overrun, and lay a wash basin on the lectern. All of her students gathered closer to observe. Then she'd begin to scrub her hands, lifting them high for our inspection as the rivulets wiggled down her forearms and disappeared into her sleeves. If she spoke at all it was softly and with great difficulty. At the conclusion of the hour she'd dry her hands on her blotter and empty the basin in a desk drawer."

As Professor Amory's article helped us to see, during the Deep Silence we were discovering arithmetic. "742 + $2^1/_4$ - 3.14/\$.25 = $744^1/_4$ - 3.14/\$.25," we explain on page $\sqrt{2}$ and from there proceed to our ingenious elaboration, "All/ one, All/one, All/one." Because meaning is water, 2=also=toward=you(tu)=half a ballerina's skirt, but thought is number and hence, $\mu_e = f(W_e)$ is equivalent to our first sentence, "We think me," regardless of carbuncles, eyebrows or talk of tides. This accounts for Dr. Schleeter-Nachter's "hypothesisettes," the prominence of the Algebra of Mud and the Variorum's twelve volume format. There can be margins but no boundary.

Careful readers may notice that only the first sentence remains unchanged from the previous editions of this work. Through exhaustive, computer-assisted analysis, Professor Cuda has isolated all manuscript fragments originating from our Deep Silence and demonstrated that, had we lived, we would have entirely repudiated our former thinking. Dr. Irwin himself has conceded that the present volume "has no relationship to Dr. Stitz's writings at all!" Our insights have forced us to continue beyond the manuscripts, beyond the dead letter, beyond "Myra Stitz." Even where the words are identical, the thought is wholly new. Our children know we are at every point the same.

As always, we encourage all imaginative response. However, we hope our detractors will forego the quibbles that in the past have been so detrimental to lively conversation.

Many persons have a great stake in misunderstanding. So often criticism of our work has evinced the character of blindness resisting its own reflection. Myra Stitz is not to be feared. May our critics learn to become one another. The four editions are the work of one author.

> A. B. C.
> R. F. D.
> L. S. A.
> S. S. S.
> P. S-N.
> with D. U. I.
> Meridian College

Interface of the Cosmic Edition

Thought lives richly in the moment of the end. It leans, ready to topple upon its own consummation. Become the empty page. Yesterday was Speech, Earth, Author, Number. Today we are the russet house wren beneath the green awning above this shattered window. What tree is this whose branches would enfold me? Enwing yourself; become Sky. Our bowels tighten: no more words.

Once more I appear before you, my friends, daughters, lovers, sons, to instruct you in Stitzsong. When in distant time we were kissed by the grill of the frenetic delivery van and from the deep green naughtness sucked Mother-Death, our power misled us. We believed in direction, in shape. Now it is the eighth day, and there have been many editions. Irwinfaith overwhelms Drewstory. In SSS and the propositions Schleeter-Nachter has bloomed. So much has moved outward, and now we return to you, O Meridian, our navel. But no more words.

Sing!

It is in the odor of cigars, the dry foam rings on yesternight's glasses of stout, in this café that worlds us round, our Library, that Myra appears. She formed you *ex nihilo* of campus grass and canal slime, comely beings, to walk in this garden of mind. Livid flowers rise from other pages, other names. Dimly seen creatures encircle us, and upon the canal, the barges drifting, the grain bins silent with fallow stench, we know our thought has been too small. All is written to be forgot. Everything is authorized. This preface contains no edition....

M. Q. S.
via lactea

Face

Myra Stitz is dead.

Although it is now commonplace to consign Myra Q. Stitz to the realm of myth and *Refractions of Identity* to that of hoax and folly, even to speak casually of Dr. Stitz's nonexistence, I want to make a few remarks about the woman I knew. Or thought I knew. I have no desire to engage in partisan debate. I've lived long enough to know memory is evidence of nothing.

Nearly twenty years ago an article on the relationship of societal to textual corruption appeared in the unusually short-lived *Journal of Anachronisms* (vol. I, no. i). The author, one Dudley Spavin, argued that the Western intelligentsia's inability "to think a single coherent thought" was the result of a conspiracy of "Trismegistians" (the term has not stuck) to deny that anything is simply itself. "A stop sign's a stop sign, isn't it?" he argued in his spirited style. Spavin's article proposed a return to logical positivism, free enterprise and a modified feudalism. It did not cause a stir.

However, it did provoke a response by Peter Schleeter-Nachter who receives credit for being first to observe that "deterioration" is the one concept utterly alien to Stitzian thinking. For years the critics of *Refractions of Identity* had been frustrated by the tendency of Myra Stitz's writing to incorporate its antagonists. Every new attack on *Refractions* became the starting point for the next edition. Every articulate opponent was invited to head the geometrically expanding editorial board. Eventually the institutional rewards for such invitations became substantial. As Schleeter-Nachter observed, Stitzism threatened to become a discipline in itself, a force capable of subjugating the entire academy, even a synonym for intellectual life. In the concluding paragraph of his article (which appeared in *Eidos* just two months before his startling suicide), Dr. Schleeter-Nachter observed that by failing to acknowledge its own extinction, the entire corpus of Stitziana may have become seriously degenerate: "Not the flowering of thought but rottenness at its very root. A progressive estrangement from the primordial silence."

Almost immediately revisionists began to turn Myra Stitz against herself as critics re-examined what Schleeter-Nachter had termed "the inadequate ontology of Nothing." Old doubts reappeared with new authority. Editorial license now became "insufficient respect for the definitive lacunae"; fraud became "naive unawareness of their own substantialist tropes." The radical notion of identity on which the editors had based their work was revealed to be a jejune logocentrism: "Thought doesn't *grow*; there just gets to be more of it." And, finally, the illusion of coherency that had bound together the marginalia, library cards and bric-a-brac into a life was dispelled. "If no one had bothered to argue about Myra Stitz," one commentator observed, "she never would have existed at all."

Although Meridian College does show an "M. Q. Stitz" on its faculty some four decades ago, her appointment seems to have been in Zoology (!), and, aside from the unreliable memoirs and letters amassed by Dr. Stitz's editors, few college documents mention her. A single photograph, badly faded, in the *Meridian College Standard* shows her square nose, cropped hair, and distracted gaze (the view of her mouth is obstructed by a plump cheerleader's hip) riding atop a Science Club homecoming float, and a few surviving minutes of administrative meetings list her as second on motions to computerize the faculty-staff payroll. Her name appears in variant spellings (Moira Stitz and M. Q. Stitts) on two of the four articles attributed to her (only one of which deals with any subject related to *Refractions*), and on the single legal document in the county records office—a Quit Claim Deed on a vacant lot used for trash disposal five miles from town— her address is recorded beneath the bizarre orthography "Miracue Stizz." Even the notes and paper scraps so often cited by Dr. Stitz's editors are in a variety of scripts and cover such an abundance of disconnected topics that they more easily support than refute the thesis of a loose association of distinct persons confused by accident, coincidence and, possibly, deceit.

Nor is my own experience, despite its lingering vividness, any help. The blue-walled café in which I dreamed and drank stout is a brick drive-in bank, and the grain bins that once lined the canal are miraculously absent now. The canal itself has developed an unnatural odor as of too-sweet perfume, and the college campus where I discovered a world is hardly larger than a parking lot. Even the stately Victorian home in which I thought I lived out my youth is, in reality, crumbling stucco, quite shabby, and nowhere I've ever known. Irwin, Cuda, Amory are all buried, senile, or like Drew, vanished into some dusty crack of the planet. Perhaps there was a Myra Q. Stitz, just as there surely was a Moses, an Odysseus, and a Richard III, but, if so, she was lost to me long ago in the successive nights of editorial frenzy, the chaos of index cards, triumphal illuminations.

So I have no intention of defending in my dotage causes that are lost. Myra Stitz is dead. My only wish is to underscore the aptness of Schleeter-Nachter's critique, concede the suspicions of Dr. Stitz's nay-sayers, and be done with contention once and for all. Dr. Stitz's work clearly omits Nothing entirely. In fact, extinction is so absent from *Refractions of Identity* that, without exaggeration, one could consider it the distinguishing feature of the several editions, perhaps even Dr. Stitz's principal motivation for never writing anything at all. More to the point, I think we are forced to conclude that Dr. Stitz never lived precisely so that her work, by being anything, would inevitably embody the deterioration of which she said so little. The author of *Refractions of Identity* is that same silence Dr. Schleeter-Nachter heard so clearly.

This afternoon I sat in my old classroom, listened to a bald, bearded man discuss Machiavelli's *Prince*, the ethics of deception. There was nothing so remarkable about my new position, nothing to assure me half a century had evaporated. My strongest impression was that the arthritic intruder in the last row was not me. I watched as the waves of heat from the open windows lulled the students, watched as the lethargy accumulated in the room like mold. And then I was surprised to hear a familiar phrase. "We think me," the young lecturer said. "We think..." I felt proud and rose to claim the thought, but once on my feet I merely continued out of the room. "If no one talks about us," he continued, "we grow uncertain. If no one listens, we are not there."

the function of art at the present time

Coming down the street on the left-hand sidewalk is a mime or juggler—that is, a youth in whiteface with eyes uplifted and hands poised to catch an object you can't quite see—and trotting beside him two black children in cutoffs cat-calling. A biker pedals in and out of the cars against the flow of traffic, apparently headed toward a clatch of young women, arms crossed, cackling, all dressed in hot colors—yellow, crimson, magenta, garish green. In a scene extravagant with color the green leaps out. There's a fight in progress around a car that's got one wheel up on the curb and the front doors open—an overweight, flush-faced guy in an absurd tam-o'-shanter being punched in the nose by a skinhead and his girlfriend. Nobody looks, but that could be fear. An abandoned baby stroller stands in the sun. (Empty?) A skater zips around it with a boom-box under one arm. And high above everything, a huge Schweppes billboard looms, its lettering funnel-shaped, uppercase S swooping toward the lowercase one, so the logo functions like a pointer. The word—Schweppes—means nothing, of course, but it highlights what does.

Specifically, a torso peering over a roof that, except for its silhouette against the final yellow e of the billboard, would pass unnoticed. We don't know this shadow, couldn't describe her (him?). Does she live here? No race, class, color or soul, but she's curious. She leans waaaay out—points her chin, cranes her neck—and fixes a man at a sidewalk table six stories below. It seems important to say that this man— bald with a red fringe and pallid scalp—is exactly the same size as everyone else and does nothing distinctive. He holds a pencil in one hand; his arm rests on a yellow tablet. No detail in the scene determines how to take him. If we're observing a romance—the watcher and the watched—it's deep or uncanny. Possibly the man and the silhouette are enemies. Could her posture be distrustful? But what makes the two so interesting is that he has twisted in his chair—as if startled—to stare back up at her six stories away. What has drawn him to a shadow? Their look organizes everything.

Behind the man, a waiter with one hand on a chair back rolls his sleeve and chats with a white woman in a business suit. Beside them the sidewalk is bare for a distance, except for a striped cat on a stoop. At the street's far end there's a brick wall with a huge mural.

The mural is the neighborhood—café tables, Schweppes sign (but changed from yellow to green), traffic, stroller, even the biker and cat (but calico now). The surface is turned at an oblique angle so the end with the mime—we can see now that it's a mime, not a juggler—is larger than life, and the end with the cat converges to a grayish miasma, virtual nothing. In the near corner the artist has scribbled a word, tantalizingly legible, and leaning forward we're about to make it out when the museum guard coughs loudly, embarrassing us, so we hurry away.